John Wyndham
Chocky

PENGUIN BOOKS

PENGUIN BOOKS

Published by the Penguin Group
Penguin Books Ltd, 80 Strand, London WC2R ORL, England
Penguin Group (USA) Inc., 375 Hudson Street, New York, New York 10014, USA
Penguin Group (Canada), 90 Eglinton Avenue East, Suite 700, Toronto, Ontario, Canada M4P 2Y3
(a division of Pearson Penguin Canada Inc.)
Penguin Ireland, 25 St Stephen's Green, Dublin 2, Ireland (a division of Penguin Books Ltd)
Penguin Group (Australia), 250 Camberwell Road,
Camberwell, Victoria 3124, Australia (a division of Pearson Australia Group Pty Ltd)
Penguin Books India Pvt Ltd, 11 Community Centre,
Panchsheel Park, New Delhi – 110 017, India
Penguin Group (NZ), 67 Apollo Drive, Rosedale, North Shore 0632, New Zealand
(a division of Pearson New Zealand Ltd)
Penguin Books (South Africa) (Pty) Ltd, 24 Sturdee Avenue,
Rosebank, Johannesburg 2196, South Africa

Penguin Books Ltd, Registered Offices: 80 Strand, London WC2R ORL, England

www.penguin.com

First published by Michael Joseph 1968
Published in Penguin Books 1970
Reissued in this edition 2009

009

Copyright © John Wyndham, 1968
All rights reserved

The moral right of the author has been asserted

Printed in England by Clays Ltd, Elcograf S.p.A.

ISBN: 978-0-141-04218-3

www.greenpenguin.co.uk

All persons and institutions in this story (other than Jack de Manio and the BBC) are entirely mythical

One

It was in the spring of the year that Matthew reached twelve that I first became aware of Chocky. Late April, I think, or possibly early May; anyway I am sure it was the spring because on that Saturday afternoon I was out in the garden shed unenthusiastically oiling the mower for labours to come when I heard Matthew's voice speaking close outside the window. It surprised me; I had had no idea he was anywhere about until I heard him say, on a note of distinct irritation, and apropos, apparently, of nothing:

'*I* don't know why. It's just the way things *are*.'

I assumed that he had brought one of his friends into the garden to play, and that the question which prompted his remark had been asked out of earshot. I listened for the reply, but there was none. Presently, after a pause, Matthew went on, rather more patiently:

'Well, the time the world takes to turn round is a day, and that's twenty-four hours, and . . .'

He broke off, as if at some interruption, though it was quite inaudible to me. Then he repeated:

'I don't know *why*. And I don't see why thirty-two hours would be more sensible. Anyway, twenty-four hours do make a day, everybody knows that, and seven days make a week . . .' Again he appeared to be cut short. Once more he protested. 'I don't see why seven is a sillier number than eight . . .'

Evidently there was another inaudible interruption, then he went on: 'Well, who wants to divide a week into halves and quarters, anyway? What'd be the point of it? A week just *is* seven days. And four weeks *ought* to

7

make a month, only usually it's thirty days or thirty-one days . . .' – 'No, it's *never* thirty-two days. You've got a sort of thing about thirty-two . . .' – 'Yes, I can see that, but we *don't want* a week of eight days. Besides, the world goes round the sun in three hundred and sixty-five days, and nobody can do anything that will make that turn into proper halves and quarters.'

At that point the peculiarity of this one-sided conversation aroused my curiosity enough to make me put my head cautiously out of the open window. The garden was sunny, and that side of the shed was sheltered and warm. Matthew was seated on an upturned seed-tray, leaning back against the brick wall of the shed just under the window, so that I was looking down on the top of his fair-haired head. He seemed to be gazing straight across the lawn and into the bushes beyond. There was no sign of a companion, nor of any place one could be hidden.

Matthew, however, went on:

'There are twelve of these months in a year, so . . .' He broke off again, his head a little tilted as though he were listening. I listened, too, but there was not a whisper of any other voice to be heard.

'It's *not* just stupid,' he objected. 'It's like that because no kind of same-sized months would fit into a year properly, even if . . .'

He broke off once more, but this time the source of the interruption was far from inaudible. Colin, the neighbour's boy, had shouted from the next garden. Matthew's air of preoccupation dropped away instantly. He jumped up with a friendly answering whoop, and ran off across the lawn towards the gap in the dividing hedge.

I turned back to my oiling, puzzled, but reassured by the sound of normal boyish noises from next door.

I put the incident out of my mind for the time being, but it recurred to me that evening when the children had

8

both gone upstairs to bed, and I found myself vaguely troubled by it. Not so much by the conversation – for, after all, there is nothing unusual in any child holding muttered exchanges with him, or her, self – as by the form of it: the consistency of its assumption that a second party was involved, and the improbable subject for argument. I was prompted after a time to ask:

'Darling, have you noticed anything odd – no, I don't exactly mean odd – anything unusual, about Matthew lately?'

Mary lowered her knitting, and looked at me over it.

'Oh, so *you* have, have you? Though I agree "odd" isn't exactly the word. Was he listening to nothing or talking to himself?'

'Talking – well, both really,' I said. 'How long has this been going on?'

She considered.

'The first time I noticed it would be – oh, I suppose about two or three weeks ago.'

I nodded. It did not greatly surprise me that I had not encountered Matthew in the mood before. I saw little of either of the children during the week. She went on:

'It didn't seem worth bothering about. Just another of those crazes children get, you know. Like the time when he was being a car, and had to steer himself round corners, and change gear on hills, and put on the brake whenever he stopped. Fortunately, that wore off quite soon. Probably this will, too.'

There was more hope than conviction in her tone.

'You're not worried about him?' I asked.

She smiled.

'Oh, good gracious, no. He's perfectly well. What I am more worried about is us.'

'Us?'

'Well, it begins to look to me rather as if we may have got another Piff, or something like her, in the family.'

I felt, and probably looked, dismayed. I shook my head.

'Oh, no! Don't say it. Not another Piff!' I protested.

Mary and I had met sixteen years before, and had married a year later.

Our meeting had been, according to the view one takes of these things, either entirely fortuitous, or else worked out with an unnecessarily cunning deviousness by destiny. At any rate there had been nothing conventional about it; and as far as either of us could recollect we had never been introduced.

It was the year in which, as a reward for several previous years' conscientious application to duty, I had risen to the status of junior partner in the firm of Ainslie and Tallboy, Chartered Accountants, of Bedford Square. At this distance of time I am not sure whether it was celebration of the achievement, or the fading effect of the work that had led to it, which determined me to spend my summer holidays as far from my routine concerns as I could get. Probably it was a bit of both. At any rate, the urge to fresh woods and pastures new was strongly upon me.

The world was, in theory, open to me. In practice, however, it was narrowed by considerations of cost, the time available, and the travel allowance then in force, until it appeared not to extend beyond Europe. Still, there is quite a lot of Europe.

At first I toyed with the idea of an Aegean cruise. The prospect of sunlit isles set in a cerulean sea dazzled me, and there were siren songs in my ears. Unfortunately, it seemed upon investigation, all berths on such cruises except those at a prohibitive first-class rate, had been booked since the previous October.

Then I had thoughts of setting out vagabond-wise, wandering through the countryside care-and-fancy-free, but, on reflection, it seemed to me that an unknowledgeable traveller with no more linguistic equipment than indifferent schoolboy French would be unlikely to make the best use of the limited time.

This brought me, as it has brought many thousands of others, to considering the merits of a tour. After all, one would be guided through many interesting places on the way. I reconsidered Greece, and discovered it would take a long time to get there and back by road, even at hundreds of miles a day. In the end, I reluctantly postponed the glories of Greece for exploration at a future date, and contemplated the grandeurs of Rome, which were, it seemed, much more readily available.

For Mary Bosworth that had been a time of hiatus. She had come down from London University with, she hoped, a degree in history, and was still wondering how best she could employ it – if, indeed, she had it. With her friend, Melissa Campley, she decided that, after the constrictions of exam syllabuses, the gap might be filled by a holiday abroad which would expand their minds. There was some difference of opinion on the location most likely to do this efficiently. Mary had favoured the idea of Yugoslavia which was then cautiously setting its door more ajar to tourists from the West. Melissa had inclined to Rome as the destination, partly because she disapproved of Communism, on principle, but more because she envisaged the journey to Rome as a form of pilgrimage. Mary's doubts on the validity of a pilgrimage conducted by tourist coach she brushed aside. Such a pilgrimage, with a guide to improve your knowledge of the world as you travelled was, she pointed out, certainly no less valid, and in several ways more commendable, than a pilgrimage by cavalcade enlivened en route with dubious stories. The argument had eventually been settled by the travel agency when it warned Mary of mysterious delays in the granting of Yugoslavian visas just then. So Rome it was to be.

Two days before they were due to leave Melissa went down with mumps. Mary, after ringing up a number of friends and finding none of them willing to take Melissa's place at such short notice, had eventually, and somewhat reluctantly, presented herself to take her place, unaccompanied, on a tour not of her own choice.

Thus, it was by a series of hitches and second-bests that Mary and I, with twenty-five others, had come to form the complement of a startling pink and orange coach which, with the words GOPLACES TOURS LTD in gleaming golden letters on its sides, trundled us southwards across Europe.

We never got to Rome.

After spending an uncomfortable night at an indifferent hotel a few miles from Lake Como, where the accommodation was inadequate and the food disagreeable, we woke one benign-looking morning with the sun just clearing the mist from the Lombardy hills, to find ourselves stranded. Our courier, our driver, and our coach itself had all vanished overnight.

An agitated counsel resulted in the sending of an urgent telegram to the head-office of GOPLACES TOURS LTD. It brought no reply.

During the course of the day tempers deteriorated, not only those of the tourists, but of the hotel proprietor as well. He had, it appeared, another coach-party booked for that night. The party duly arrived, and chaos took over.

In the disputes which followed it became obvious that Mary and I, the only two unattached members of our party, were not going to stand a chance of beds, so we, during the evening, bagged two moderately easy chairs in the restaurant, and stuck to them. They were at least better than sleeping on the floor.

By the following morning there was still no answer from GOPLACES. A second, and more urgent, message was dispatched.

After some delay we managed to get coffee and rolls.

'This,' I said to Mary as we breakfasted, 'is not going to get us anywhere.'

'What do you think has happened?' she asked.

I shrugged. 'At a guess I'd say Goplaces has gone bust, that our two were tipped off about it somehow, and chose the opportunity to make off with the coach in order to flog it.'

'You mean it's no good our waiting here?'

'Not a bit, I'd say.' I let that register, and then asked: 'Have you got any money?'

'Not enough to get home with, I'm afraid. About five or six pounds, and nearly four thousand lire. I didn't expect to need anything much,' she said.

'Nor me. I've got about ten, and a few lira. What do you say to seeing what we can do?'

She looked round. Every other member of our party within sight seemed to be engaged in ill-tempered argument, or oppressed by gloom.

'All right,' she agreed.

We set out, carrying our suitcases, and sat by the roadside until a bus came along. In the small town which was its destination we found a railway station, and took tickets for Milan. The consul there did not welcome us, but eventually he relaxed enough to advance us the money to cover our fares home, second class.

We married the following spring. It turned out to be quite an affair. There were so many Bosworths that I had a feeling of being engulfed.

My own father and mother had both been dead some years, and I have few close relatives so that the Gore side of the ceremony was supported only scantily by my best man, Alan Froome, an uncle and aunt, a couple of cousins, my senior partner, and a scatter of friends. The Bosworth assembly practically filled the rest of the church. As well as Mary's parents there were her eldest sister Janet, with her husband and her four children, displaying evidence that there would soon be a fifth; her next eldest sister, Patience, with her three; her brothers, Edward (Ted) and Francis (Frank) with their wives and seemingly innumerable children; a host of uncles, aunts, and cousins, and a mob of friends and acquaintances all apparently gifted with such fecundity that the place resembled a combined infant school and crèche. My father-in law, having no further daughters to dispose of, was minded to do the occasion in style, and did – exhaustingly.

It was with a feeling akin to convalescence that we caught up with the previous year's intentions of spending our honeymoon partly in Yugoslavia, and partly amid the Grecian isles.

From it we came back to take up residence in a small house in Cheshunt – a strategic position for easy contact with most elements of the Bosworth ganglion.

Even when we were buying the house I had, I recall, a slight sense of misgiving, an intimation that I was not taking the wisest course, but at the time I put it down to my own prejudice. I was unfamiliar with clan life, I had not been brought up to it, and what I had seen of it had little appeal, but for Mary's sake I determined to do my best to qualify as an acceptable associate member. She was accustomed to it. Moreover, I told myself, it would help her to feel less lonely while I was away from home.

The intention was good, but as things turned out it was a mistake. It soon became clear to me, and, I fear, to most of the rest, that I am not first-class clan material – though, even so, I suppose I might in time have found myself a niche among them had it not been for other factors . . .

During our first year there Mary's sister Janet produced her fifth, and was heard to speak in favour of six as a good round number. Her other sister, Patience, was well on the way to completing her quartet, an additional aunthood was thrust upon Mary by her brother Frank, and she received several invitations to act as godmother. But she had failed to detect any indication that there was to be a baby of her own.

Our second wedding anniversary approached and

passed, still without any sign. Mary consulted another doctor, and, unconvinced by him, appealed to a specialist. He, too, told her there was nothing for her to worry about . . . but worry she did.

I, for my own part, felt no great urgency. We were both young, we had plenty of time before us: where was the need for hurry? Indeed, I did not dislike the idea of a few more years of freedom before we trammelled ourselves with family cares, and said as much to Mary.

She agreed, but unconvincingly. She contrived to give the impression that it was sweet of me to pretend not to mind when she knew I did. I could not press the point further for fear of seeming to protest too much.

I don't understand women. Nobody does. Least of all themselves. I don't know, and nor do they, for instance, how far this compulsion that most of them have to produce a baby as soon as possible after marriage is attributable to a straight biological urge, and what percentages of it can be more justly credited to other factors such as conformity with peoples' expectations, the desire to prove that one is normal, the belief that it will establish status, a sense of personal achievement, the symbol of one's maturity, a feeling of solidarity, the obligation of holding one's own in competition with the neighbours. Nevertheless, whatever the proportions of these ingredients, and other trace-elements, they compound to build up a formidable pressure. It is not the least use pointing out that some of the world's most influential women, Elizabeth the First, Florence Nightingale, for instance, would actually have *lost* status had they become mums, in fact it is much wiser not to try. Babies, in a world that already has far too many, remain desirable.

It began to worry me a lot.

'She frets about it,' I confided to Alan Froome, who had been my best man. 'It's not necessary. The specialist assures her that there's nothing wrong – me, too. The confounded thing is this constant social pressure all the time. The whole family circle is baby-ridden; they talk and think about nothing else. Her sisters keep on having them, so do her brothers' wives, and all her married friends, and every time it happens it rubs it in that she doesn't. Each new baby that comes along makes her feel more inadequate and inferior until I don't know, and I'm sure she no longer knows, how much she wants a baby for itself, and how far it has become a sort of challenge. All the time she's over a sort of forced draught. She's in a circle where it's a kind of competition in which every married woman is considered ipso facto an entrant – which makes it damned hard on a non-starter.

'It might not matter so much if she were the independent sort, but she isn't really. She's happier conforming, and the pressure to conform is terrific – only she can't. . . . The whole thing is getting her down – and that's getting me down . . .'

Alan said:

'Do you think you're getting quite the right slant on this, old man? I mean, does it matter how far her desire for a baby is inherent, and how much it is being stepped up by the environment? Surely, the point is that she has it – and has it very strongly. It seems to me there's only one thing to be done about that.'

'But, damn it, we've tried; and we've taken just about all the advice there is . . .'

'Well, then it looks to me as if the only thing you can do is take the alternative, don't you think?'

So we had adopted Matthew.

For a time he seemed to be the answer. Mary adored him, and he certainly gave her plenty to do. And he enabled her to talk babies on an equal footing with the rest.

Or was it? Well, not quite, perhaps. . . . She began to get an impression that some babies confer a little more equality than other babies. And when the first thrill of her excitement had worn off she became aware of a feeling that her association with the motherhood group was a shade, just a shade, less than that of a member in full standing. It was all conveyed by the nicest, almost indetectably refined blend of sympathy and bitchiness . . .

'We're moving,' I told Alan about six months later.

He looked at me for a moment, eyebrows raised.

'Where to?' he inquired.

'I've found a place at Hindmere, Surrey. A nice house, slightly bigger, more countrified. Stands higher. Said to be better air there.'

He nodded.

'I see,' he said, and nodded again. 'Good idea.'

'What do you see?'

'It's the other side. The whole width of London in between. . . . What does Mary think about it?'

'Not enthusiastic – she's not very enthusiastic about anything these days – but she's perfectly willing to give it a trial.' I paused, and then added: 'It seemed to me the only thing to do. I had a nasty feeling she might be heading for a breakdown. It'll get her out of the influence. Leave that family of hers to wallow in its own fecundity. Give her the chance to make a start on her own footing. In a new place nobody will know that Matthew isn't her own child unless she chooses to tell them. I think she's beginning to realize that.'

'Best thing you could do,' Alan agreed.

It undoubtedly was. It put new life into Mary. Within a few weeks she had started to take herself in hand, to join things and make new acquaintances, to take a place in her own right.

Furthermore, within a year of the move there had come the first harbinging signs that a baby was on the way.

It was I who later broke the news to Matthew, now aged two, that he had a new baby sister. Rather to my concern he immediately burst into tears. With some difficulty I elicited that what he had really hoped for was a baby lamb. However, he managed the readjustment quite easily, and quickly adopted an attitude of responsibility towards Polly.

We then became a comfortable and contented family of four – save for the interlude when we appeared to be five, because we had Piff, as well.

Two

Piff was a small, or supposedly small, invisible friend that Polly had acquired when she was about five. And while she lasted she was a great nuisance.

One would start to sit down upon a conveniently empty chair only to be arrested in an unstable and inelegant pose by a cry of anguish from Polly; one had, it seemed, been about to sit on Piff. Any unexpected movement, too, was liable to bowl over the intangible Piff who would then be embraced and comforted by a lot of sympathetic muttering about careless and brutal daddies.

Frequently, and more likely than not when a knockout seemed imminent, or the television play had reached the brink of its denouement, there would come an urgent call from Polly's bedroom above; the cause had to be investigated although the odds were about four to one that it would concern Piff's dire need of a drink of water. We would sit down at a table for four in a café, and there would be agonized appeals to a mystified waitress for an extra chair for Piff. I could be in the act of releasing my clutch when a startling yell would inform me that Piff was not yet with us, and the car door had to be opened to let her aboard. Once I testily refused to wait for her. It was not worth it; my heartlessness had clouded our whole day.

Piff, for one of her kind, had been remarkably diurnal. She must have been with us the best part of a year – and it seemed a great deal longer – but in the end she somehow got mislaid during our summer holiday. Polly, much taken up with several more substantial, and much more audible, new friends, dropped Piff with great callousness, and she was still missing on our return journey.

Once I was satisfied that she was not going to follow and take up residence with us again I was able to feel quite sorry for the deserted Piff, apparently doomed to wander for ever in summer's traces upon the forlorn beaches of Sussex; nevertheless, her absence came as a great relief – even, one suspected, to Polly herself. The idea that we might now have acquired another such was by no means welcome.

'A grim thought,' said I, 'but, fortunately improbable, I think. A Piff can provide useful bossing material for a member of the younger female age-groups, but an eleven-year-old boy who wants to boss seems to me more likely to take it out on other, and smaller boys.'

'I'm sure I hope you're right,' Mary said, but dubiously. 'One Piff was more than enough.'

'There's quite a different quality here,' I pointed out. 'If you remember, Piff spent about eighty per cent of her time being scolded for something or other, and having to take it. This one appeared to be criticizing, and coming back with opinions of its own.'

Mary looked startled.

'What *do* you mean? I don't see how . . .'

I repeated, as nearly as I could recall, the one-sided conversation I had overheard.

Mary frowned as she considered it.

'I don't understand that at all,' she said.

'Oh, it's simple enough. After all the arrangement of a calendar is just a convention . . .'

'But that's just what it isn't – not to a child, David. To an eleven-year-old it seems like a natural law – just as much as day and night, or the seasons. . . . A week is a week, and it has seven days – it's an unquestionable provision, it just *is so*.'

'Well, that's more or less what Matthew was saying, *but* apparently he was being argued with – *or* he was arguing with himself. In either case it isn't easy to explain.'

'He must have been arguing with what someone's told him at school – one of his teachers, most likely.'

'I suppose so,' I conceded. 'All the same, it's a new one on me. I've heard of calendar reformers who want all months to have twenty-eight days, but never of anyone advocating an eight-day week – or, come to that a thirty-two day month.' I pondered a moment. 'Besides, it just doesn't begin to be on. For one thing you'd need nineteen more days in a year . . .' I shook my head. 'Anyway,' I went on, 'I don't mean to make heavy weather of it. It just strikes me as odd. I wondered if you had noticed anything of the sort, too.'

Mary lowered her knitting again, and studied its pattern thoughtfully.

'No – well, not exactly. I have heard him muttering to himself occasionally, but nearly all children do that at times. I'm afraid I didn't pay any attention – actually I was anxious not to do anything which might encourage another Piff. But there is one thing: the questions he's been asking lately – '

'Lately!' I repeated. 'Was there ever a time when he didn't?'

'I know. But these are a bit different. I mean – well, usually his questions have been average-boy questions.'

'I hadn't noticed they'd changed.'

'Oh, the old kind keep on, but there's a new kind, too – with a different – a different sort of slant.'

'Such as . . . ?'

'Well, one of them was about why are there two sexes? He said he didn't see why it was necessary to have two people to produce one, so how had it got arranged that way, and why? That's a difficult one, you know, on the spur of the moment – well, it's difficult anyway, isn't it?'

I frowned. 'Um – now you come to mention it. . . . Of course, it does sort of help to – er – spread the load . . .' I tried, doubtfully.

'But I didn't mention it: Matthew did. And there was another one, too, about "where is Earth?" Now, I ask you – where *is* Earth? – in relation to what? Oh, yes, he knows it goes round the sun, but where, please, is the sun? And, there were some others – simply not his kind of questions.'

I appreciated her point. Matthew's questions were plentiful, and quite varied, but they usually kept a more homely orbit: things like 'Why do you use a washer with a nut?' or, 'Why can't we live on grass if horses can?'

'A new phase?' I suggested. 'He's reached a stage where things are beginning to widen out for him.'

Mary shook her head, giving me a look of reproach.

'That, darling, is what I've been telling you. What I want to know is *why* they should widen, and his interests apparently change, quite so suddenly.'

'But why not? What do you expect? Isn't it what children go to school for – to have their minds widened and their interests expanded?'

'I know,' she said, frowning again. 'But that's not quite it, David. This doesn't seem to me like just development. It's more as if he'd switched to a different track. It's a sudden change in quality – quality and approach.' She went on frowning for the pause before she added: 'I do wish we knew a little more about his parents. That might help. In Polly I can see bits of you and bits of me. It gives one a feeling of something to go on. But with Matthew there's no guide at all. . . . There's nothing to give me any idea what to expect . . .'

I could see what she meant – though I have my reservations about the validity of this ability to see parent in child. I could also see where we were heading. In about three more moves we'd be back at the old unprofitable contest: heredity versus environment. To sidestep that I said:

'It looks to me as if the best thing we can do for the present is simply to listen and watch carefully – though not obviously – until we get a firmer impression. It's no good worrying ourselves over what may easily be an insignificant passing phase.'

And there we decided to leave it for the time being.

But only briefly. I collected my next specimen the following day.

For our Sunday afternoon walk Matthew and I had chosen the river bank.

I had not mentioned to him the conversation I had overheard, and did not intend to. But as a result of it, and of my talk with Mary, I observed Matthew with more attention than usual. It was not well rewarded. As far as I could tell he seemed to be quite his ordinary self. I wondered if he were not a shade more noticing, showing ever so slightly more awareness of the things about us ... I couldn't be sure. I suspected it of being subjective – simply that I was being more noticing and aware of things about Matthew. I could not detect any significant variation of his interests and questions – not until we had been going for half an hour and were passing below Five Elms Farm ...

The path there led us through a field where a couple of dozen cows blankly eyed us on our way. Only then did Matthew take a swerve off his usual beat. We were almost across the field, just a little short of the stile in the far side hedge, when he slowed to a halt, and stood there, regarding the nearest cow seriously. The cow looked back at Matthew, with a tinge of disquiet, I thought. After he and the cow had contemplated one another for a few moments Matthew asked:

'Daddy, why is it a cow stops?'

It sounded at first like a why-does-a-chicken-cross-the-road question, but as he asked it Matthew continued to study the cow with great concentration. The animal appeared to find this embarrassing. It started to swing its head from side to side without taking its glassy eyes off his face. I decided to take the question straight.

'How do you mean?' I inquired. 'Why does it stop what?'

'Well, it gets a bit of the way, but then it doesn't seem

able to get any further, ever. I don't see why not . . .'

I was still out of touch.

'A bit of the way where?' I asked him.

The cow lost interest, and decided to move away. Matthew watched it thoughtfully as it went.

'What I mean is,' he explained, 'when old Albert comes to the yard gate there, all the cows understand that it's milking time. They all know which stall to go to in the shed, and they understand about waiting there until they've been milked. Then, when it's over and Albert opens the gate again, they understand about going back into the field. But there they just stop. I don't see why.'

I was beginning to get his drift.

'You mean they just stop understanding?' I tried.

'Yes,' Matthew agreed. 'You see, they don't *want* to stay in this field, because if they can find a gap in the hedge they get out. So, if they want to go out why don't they just open the gate for themselves and go out that way? They could, easily.'

'Well, they – they don't know how to open it,' I said.

'That's just it, Daddy. Why don't they understand how to open it? They've watched Albert do it hundreds of times – every time they've been milked. They've got brains enough to remember which stall to go to; why can't they remember how Albert opens the gate? I mean if they understand some things, why not a simple thing like that? What is it that doesn't go on happening inside their heads so that they stop?'

That led us on to the question of limited intelligence which was a concept that baffled him entirely.

He could grasp the idea of no intelligence. You just hadn't got it. But once you had it, how could it be limited? Surely if you went on applying and applying even a little intelligence it might take a longish time, but it *must* come up with the answer sooner or later. How could there possibly be such things as boundary lines to intelligence?

It was a discussion that continued for the rest of our

walk, by the time we got home I had a good idea of what Mary had meant. It was not the sort of inquiry – and by no means the sort of subsequent debate – that one associated with Matthew. She agreed, when I reported it to her, that I had collected quite a good specimen.

It was about ten days after that that we first heard about Chocky. It might well have been longer had Matthew not picked up some fluey germ at school which caused him to run quite a temperature for a while. When it was at its height he rambled a bit, with all defences down. There were times when he did not seem to know whether he was talking to his mother, or his father, or to some mysterious character he called Chocky. Moreover, this Chocky appeared to worry him, for he protested several times.

On the second evening his temperature ran high. Mary called down to me to come up. Poor Matthew looked in a sorry state. His colour was high, his brow damp, and he was very restless. He kept rolling his head from side to side on the pillow, almost as if he were trying to shake it free of something. In a tone of weary exasperation he said: 'No, no, Chocky. Not now. I can't understand. I want to go to sleep. . . . No. . . . Oh, do shut up and go away. . . . No, I can't tell you now . . .' He rolled his head again, and pulled his arms from under the bedclothes to press his hands over his ears. 'Oh, do stop it, Chocky. *Do* shut up!'

Mary reached across and put her hand on his forehead. He opened his eyes and became aware of her.

'Oh, Mummy, I'm so tired. Do tell Chocky to go away. She doesn't understand. She won't leave me alone . . .'

Mary glanced questioningly at me. I could only shrug and shake my head. She sat down on the side of the bed, propped Matthew up a little, and held a glass of orange juice for him to drink.

'There,' she said. 'Now lie down, darling, and try to go to sleep.'

Matthew lay back.

'I *want* to go to sleep, Mummy. But Chocky doesn't understand. He will keep on talking. Please make him shut up.'

Mary laid her hand on his forehead again.

'There now,' she soothed him. 'You'll feel better when you wake up.'

'But do *tell* him, Mummy. He won't listen to me. Tell him to go away now.'

Mary hesitated, and glanced at me again. This time it was she who shrugged. Then she rose to the occasion. Turning back, she addressed herself to a point slightly above Matthew's head. I recognized the technique she had sometimes used with Piff. In a kindly but firm tone she said:

'Chocky, you really must let Matthew be quiet and rest. He isn't at all well, Chocky, and he needs to go to sleep. So please go away and leave him alone now. Perhaps, if he's better tomorrow, you can come back then.'

'See?' said Matthew. 'You've got to clear out, Chocky, so that I can get better.' He seemed to listen. 'Yes,' he said decisively.

It appeared to work. In fact it did work.

He lay back again, and visibly relaxed.

'She's gone,' he announced.

'That's fine. Now you can settle down,' said Mary.

And he did. He wriggled into a comfortable position and lay quiet. Presently his eyes closed. In a very few minutes he was fast asleep. Mary and I looked at one another. She tucked his bedclothes closer, and put the bell-push handy. We tiptoed to the door, turned off the room light, and went downstairs.

'Well,' I said, 'what are we supposed to make of that?'

'Aren't they astonishing?' said Mary. 'Dear, oh dear, it does very much look as if this family *is* landed with another Piff.'

26

I poured us some sherry, handed Mary hers, and raised mine.

'Here's to hoping it turns out to be less of a pest than the last one,' I said. I set down the glass, and looked at it. 'You know,' I told her, 'I can't help feeling there's something wrong about this. As I said before, Piffs aren't unusual with little girls, but I don't remember hearing of an eleven-year-old boy inventing one. .... It seems out of order, somehow. .... I must ask someone about it . . .'

Mary nodded agreement.

'Yes,' she said, 'but what strikes me as even odder is – did you notice? – he doesn't seem to be clear in his own mind whether his Chocky is a him or a her. Children are usually very positive about that. They feel it's important . . .'

'I wouldn't say the feeling of importance is entirely restricted to children,' I told her, 'but I see what you mean, and you're perfectly right, of course. It *is* odd. .... The whole thing's odd . . .'

Matthew's temperature was down the next morning. He picked up quickly. In a few days he was fully recovered, and about again. So too, apparently, was his invisible friend, undiscouraged by the temporary banishment.

Now that Chocky's existence was out of the bag – and largely, I was inclined to think, because neither Mary nor I had displayed incredulity – Matthew gained enough confidence to be a little more forthcoming about him/her.

To begin with, at any rate, he/she seemed a considerable improvement on the original Piff. There was none of that business of him/her invisibly occupying one's chair, or feeling sick in teashops to which Piff had been so prone. Indeed, Chocky quite markedly lacked physical attributes. He/she appeared to be scarcely more than a presence, having perhaps something in common with Wordsworth's cuckoo, but with the added limitation that his/her wandering voice was audible to Matthew alone.

27

And intermittently, at that. There were days when Matthew seemed to forget him/her altogether. Unlike Piff, he/she was not given to cropping up any-and-everywhere, nor did he/she show any of Piff's talent for embarrassment such as a determined insistence on being taken to the lavatory in the middle of the sermon. On the whole, if one had to choose between the two intangibles, my preference was decidedly in favour of Chocky.

Mary was less certain.

'Are we,' she suddenly demanded one evening, staring into the loops of her knitting with a slight squint, 'are we, I wonder, doing the right thing in playing up to this nonsense? I know you shouldn't crush a child's imagination, and all that, but what nobody tells you is how far is enough. There comes a stage when it begins to get a bit like conspiracy. I mean, if everyone goes around pretending to believe in things that aren't there, how on earth is a child going to learn to distinguish what really is, from what really isn't?'

'Careful, darling,' I told her. 'You're steering close to dangerous waters. It chiefly depends on who, and how many, believe what isn't really is.'

She declined to be diverted. She went on:

'It'd be a most unfortunate thing if we were to find out later on that we're helping to stabilize a fantasy-system that we ought to be trying to dispel. Hadn't we better consult a psychiatrist about it? He could at least tell us whether it's one of the expectable things, or not.'

'I'm rather against making too much of it,' I told her. 'More inclined to leave it for a bit. After all we managed to lose Piff in the end, and no harm done.'

'I didn't mean send him to a psychiatrist. I thought just an inquiry on general lines to find out whether it is unusual, or simply nothing to bother about. I'd feel easier if we knew.'

'I'll ask around if you like,' I said. 'I don't think it's serious. It seems to me a bit like fiction – we *read* our kind of fiction, children often make up their own, and live it.

The thing that does trouble me a bit about it is that this Chocky seems to have barged into the wrong age-group. I think we'll find it will fade away after a bit. If it doesn't we can consult someone about it.'

I wasn't, I admit, being quite honest when I said that. Some of Matthew's questions were puzzling me considerably – not only by their un-Matthew-like character, but because, now that Chocky's existence was acknowledged, Matthew did not always present the questions as his own. Quite frequently he would preface them with: 'Chocky says he doesn't see how . . .' or 'Chocky wants to know . . .' or 'Chocky says she doesn't understand why . . .'

I let that pass, though it seemed to me rather a childish foible for a boy of Matthew's age. What made me more uneasy was Matthew's trick of appearing to take part in any ensuing discussion merely as a go-between. He sustained the role of interpreter so well.

However, one thing at least I felt could be cleared up.

'Look here,' I told him, 'I get all confused with this he-and-she business. On grounds of grammar alone it would be easier if I knew which Chocky is.'

Matthew quite agreed.

'Yes, it would,' he said. 'I thought so, too. So I asked. But Chocky doesn't seem to know.'

'Oh,' I said. 'That's rather unusual. I mean, it's one of those things people are generally pretty sure about.'

Matthew agreed about that, too.

'But Chocky's sort of different,' he told me earnestly. 'I explained all the differences between hims and hers, but she couldn't seem to get it, somehow. That's funny because he's really frightfully clever *I* think, but all he said was that it sounded a pretty silly arrangement, and wanted to know why it's like that.'

I recalled that Mary had encountered a question along those lines. Matthew went on:

'*I* couldn't tell her why. And nobody I've asked has been much help. Do you know why, Daddy?'

'Well – er – not exactly why,' I confessed. 'It's just –

29

um – how it *is*. One of Nature's ways of managing things.'

Matthew nodded.

'That's what I tried to tell Chocky – well sort of. But I don't think I can have been very good at it because she said that even if I had got it right, and it was as silly as it sounded, there still had to be a why behind it.' He paused reflectively, and then added, with a nice blend of pique and regret: 'Chocky keeps on finding such a lot of things, quite ordinary things, silly. It gets a bit boring. He thinks animals are just a hoot. I don't see why – I mean, it isn't their fault if they're not made clever enough to know any better than they do, is it?'

We talked on for a while. I was interested and showed it, but took some pains not to appear to pump. My memories of Piff suggested that pressure brought to bear on a fantasy is more apt to produce sulks than forthcomings. From what I did learn, however, I found myself feeling a little less kindly towards Chocky. He/she gave an impression of being quite aggressively opinionated. Afterwards when I recollected the entirely serious nature of our conversation I felt some increase in uneasiness. Going back over it I realized that not once in the course of it had Matthew even hinted by a single word, or slip, that Chocky was not just as real a person as ourselves, and I began to wonder whether Mary had not been right about consulting a psychiatrist . . .

However, we did get one thing more or less tidied up: the him/her question. Matthew explained:

'Chocky does talk rather like a boy, but a lot of the time it's not about the sort of thing boys talk about – if you see what I mean. And sometimes there's a bit of – well, you know the sort of snooty way chaps' older sisters often get . . . ?'

I said I did, and after we had discussed these and a few other characteristics we decided that Chocky's balance did on the whole lean more to the F than the M, and agreed that in future, provided no strong evidence showed up in contradiction, it would be convenient to class Chocky as feminine.

Mary gave me a thoughtful look when I reported to her that that, at least, was settled.

'The point is it gives more personification if Chocky is one or the other – not just an it,' I explained. 'Puts a sort of picture in the mind which must be easier for him to cope with than just a vague, undifferentiated, disembodied something. And as Matthew feels there's not much similarity to any of the boys he knows . . .'

'You decide she's feminine because you feel it will help you and Matthew to gang up on her,' Mary declared.

'Well, really, of all the nonsensical implications I ever heard – ' I began, but I broke off and let it go. I knew by her non-listening look I would be wasting my breath. She spent a few moments in reflective silence, and emerged from it to say, a little wistfully:

'I do think being a parent must have been a lot more fun before Freud was invented. As it is, if this fantasy game doesn't clear up in a week or two we shall feel a moral, social and medical obligation to do something about it. . . . And it's such nonsense really. . . . I sometimes wonder if we aren't all of us a bit morbid about children nowadays. . . . I'm sure there are more delinquents than there used to be . . .'

'I'm for keeping him clear of psychiatrists and suchlike if we can,' I told her. 'Once you let a child get the idea he's an interesting case, you turn loose a whole new boxful of troubles.'

She was silent for some seconds. Running over in her mind, I guessed, a number of the children we knew. Then she nodded.

So there we let it rest: once more waiting a bit longer to see how it would go.

In point of fact it went rather differently from anything we had in mind.

Three

'Shut up!' I snapped suddenly. 'Shut up, both of you.' Matthew regarded me with unbelieving astonishment. Polly's eyes went wide, too. Then both of them turned to look at their mother. Mary kept her expression carefully non-committal. Her lips tightened slightly, and she shook her head at them without speaking. Matthew silently finished the pudding still on his plate, and then got up and left the room, carrying himself stiffly, with the hurt of injustice. Polly choked on her final mouthful, and burst into tears. I was not feeling sympathetic.

'What have you to cry about?' I asked her. 'You started it again, as usual.'

'Come here, darling,' said Mary. She produced a handkerchief, dabbed at the wet cheeks, and then kissed her.

'There, that's better,' she said. 'Darling, Daddy didn't mean to be unkind I'm sure, but he has told you lots of times not to quarrel with Matthew – particularly at meals – you know he has, don't you?' Polly replied only with a sniff. She looked down at her fingers twisting a button on her dress. Mary went on: 'You really must try not to quarrel so much. Matthew doesn't want to quarrel with you, he hates it. It makes things very uncomfortable for us – and, I believe you hate it, too, really. So do try, it's so much nicer for everyone if you don't.'

Polly looked up from the button.

'But I *do* try, Mummy – only I can't help it.' Her tears began to rise again. Mary gave her a hug.

'Well, you'll just have to try a little harder, darling, won't you?' she said.

Polly stood passively for a moment, then she broke away across the room, and fumbled with the door-knob.

I got up, and closed the door behind her.

'I'm sorry about that,' I said as I came back. 'In fact I'm ashamed of myself – but really ...! I don't believe we've had a meal in the last two weeks without this infernal squabbling. And it's Polly who provokes it every time. She keeps on nagging and picking at him until he has to retaliate. I don't know what's come over her: they've always got on so well together ...'

'Certainly they have,' Mary agreed '– Until quite recently,' she added.

'Another phase, I suppose,' I said. 'Children seem to be just one phase after another. Letting them get through them becomes a bit wearisome once you've grasped that the next phase is likely to be just as tedious in its own way as the last.'

'I suppose you *could* call this a phase – I hope it is,' Mary said thoughtfully. 'But it's not one confined to children.'

Her tone caused me to look at her inquiringly. She asked:

'My dear, don't you see what Polly's trouble is?'

I went on looking at her blankly. She explained.

'It is just plain, ordinary jealousy – only jealousy, of course is never ordinary to the sufferer.'

'Jealousy ...?' I repeated.

'Yes, jealousy.'

'But – of whom, of what? – I don't get it.'

'Surely that should be obvious enough. Of this Chocky, of course.'

I stared at her.

'But that's absurd. Chocky is only – well, I don't know what he, she, or it is, but it's not even real – doesn't even exist, I mean.'

'Whatever does that matter? Chocky's real enough to Matthew – and, consequently, to Polly. Polly and Matthew have always got on very well, as you said. She

33

admires him tremendously. She's always been his confidante, and his aide, and it's meant a lot to her. But now he has a new confidante. This Chocky has displaced her. She's on the outside now. I'm not in the least surprised she's jealous.'

I felt bewildered.

'Now *you're* beginning to talk as if Chocky were real.'

Mary reached for a cigarette, and lit it.

'Reality is relative. Devils, evil spirits, witches and so on became real enough to the people who believed in them. Just as God is to people who believe in Him. When people live their lives by their beliefs objective reality is almost irrelevant.

'That's why I wonder if we are doing the right thing. By playing up to Matthew we are strengthening his belief, we are helping to establish the existence of this Chocky more firmly – until now we have Polly believing in her, too – to the point of a wretched jealousy. .... It's somehow getting beyond a game of make-believe – and I don't like it. I think we ought to get advice on it before it goes further.'

I could see that this time she meant it seriously.

'All right,' I agreed. 'Perhaps it would be—' I was beginning when I was cut off by the sound of the door bell.

I went to answer it, and opened the door to find myself facing a man I knew I should have recognized. I was just beginning to get him lined up – that is, I had got as far as connecting him with the Parents' Association meeting – when he introduced himself.

'Good evening, Mr Gore. I don't expect you'll remember me. Trimble's my name. I take your Matthew for maths.'

I led him into the sitting-room. Mary joined us, and greeted him, by name.

'Good evening, Mr Trimble. Matthew's just upstairs, doing his homework, I think. Shall I call him?'

Trimble shook his head.

'Oh, no, Mrs Gore. In fact, I'd rather you didn't. It's really yourselves I wanted to see – about Matthew, of course.'

We sat him down. I produced a bottle of whisky. Trimble accepted his drink gratefully.

'Well, now, what's the trouble?' I asked.

Trimble shook his head. He said reassuringly:

'Oh, no trouble. Nothing of that kind.' He paused, and went on: 'I do hope you don't mind my calling on you like this. It's quite unofficial. To be honest, it's chiefly curiosity on my part – well, a bit more than that really. I'm puzzled.' He paused once more, and looked from me to Mary and back again. 'Is it you who is the mathematician of the family?' he asked.

I denied it.

'I'm just an accountant. Arithmetic, not mathematics.'

He turned to Mary.

'Then it must be you, Mrs Gore.'

She shook her head.

'Indeed not, Mr Trimble. I can't even get arithmetic right.'

Trimble looked surprised, and a little disappointed.

'That's funny,' he said. 'I was sure – perhaps you have a relative, or some friend, who is?'

We both shook our heads. Mr Trimble continued to look surprised.

'Well,' he said, '*somebody* has been helping – no perhaps that's not the right word – shall we say, giving your son ideas about his maths – not that I mind that,' he hurried to explain. 'Indeed, in a general way I'm all for anything that gets 'em along. But that's really the point. When a child is trying to cope simultaneously with two different methods it's more likely to confuse him than get him along ...

'I'll be frank. I won't pretend that your Matthew is one of those boys you sometimes find, with a natural quick grasp of figures. He's about average, perhaps a shade above, and he's been doing quite all right – until

35

lately. But it has seemed to me recently that someone has been trying to – well, I suppose the idea was to push him on, but the stuff he's been given isn't doing that; it's getting him mixed up.' He paused again, and added apologetically: 'With a boy with a real gift for figures it might not matter; in fact, he'd probably enjoy it. But, frankly, I think it's too much for your Matthew to grasp at the moment. It's muddling him, and that's holding him back.'

'Well, just as frankly,' I told him, 'I'm completely at a loss. Do you mean that he's trying to get ahead too fast – missing out some of the steps?'

Trimble shook his head.

'Oh, no, not that. It's more – more a conflict of systems, like – well, *something* like trying to think in two languages at the same time. At first I couldn't understand what had got out of gear. Then I managed to collar some sheets of his rough work, and get a line on it. I'll show you.'

And, with pencil and paper, he did, for more than half an hour. As an audience we disappointed him, but I managed to get a grip on some of it, and ceased to be surprised that Matthew appeared muddled. Trimble went off into realms quite beyond me, and when we eventually saw him off, it was with some relief. Still, we appreciated the concern that had brought him along to see us in his own time, and promised to do our best to find the source of Matthew's confusion.

'I don't know who it can be,' Mary said as we returned to the sitting-room. 'I can't think of anyone he sees often enough.'

'It must be one of the other boys at school who's a natural whizz at maths, and got him interested although it's a bit beyond him,' I said. 'It's certainly no one I can think of. Anyway, I'll try to find out.'

I left it until the following Saturday afternoon. Then, when Mary had taken away the tea things, and Polly, too, Matthew and I had the veranda to ourselves. I picked up a pencil and scribbled on a newspaper margin:

YNYYNNYY

'What do you reckon that means, Matthew?' I asked. He glanced at it.

'A hundred and seventy-nine,' he said.

'It seems complicated when you can just write 179,' I said. 'How does it work?'

Matthew explained the binary code to me, much as Trimble had.

'But do you find that way easier?' I asked.

'Only sometimes – and it does make division difficult,' Matthew told me.

'It seems such a long way round. Wouldn't it be simpler to stick to the ordinary way?' I suggested.

'Well, you see, that's the way I have to use with Chocky because that's the way she counts,' Matthew explained. 'She doesn't understand the ordinary way, and she thinks it's silly to have to bother with ten different figures just because you've ten fingers, when all you really need is two fingers.'

I continued to look at the paper while I thought how to go on. So Chocky was in on this – I might have known . . .

'You mean when Chocky counts she just talks Ys and Ns?' I inquired.

'Sort of – only not actually. What I mean is, *I* just call them Y and N for Yes and No, because it's easier.'

I was still wondering how best to handle this new incursion of the Chocky element, but apparently I looked merely baffled, for Matthew went on to explain, patiently.

'See Daddy. A hundred is YYNNYNN and because each one is double the one on its right that means, if you start from the right hand end 1 – No, 2 – No, 4 – yes, 8 – No, 16 – No, 32 – yes, 64 – yes. You just add the Yesses together, and it's a hundred. You can get any number that way.'

I nodded.

'Yes, I see, Matthew. But, tell me, where did you first come across this way of doing it?'

'I just told you, Daddy. It's the way Chocky always uses.'

Once more I was tempted to call the Chocky bluff, but I put a thumb on my impatience. I said, reasonably:

'But she must have got it from somewhere. Did she find it in a book, or something?'

'I don't know. I expect somebody taught her,' Matthew told me, vaguely.

I recalled one or two other mathematical queries that Trimble had raised, and put them, as far as I understood them. I was scarcely surprised to learn that they, too, were devices that Chocky was accustomed to use.

So there we were, at an impasse. I was just about to end the rather fruitless session when Matthew stopped me, disturbingly. He emerged from silent reflection, as if he had made up his mind to something. With a somewhat troubled expression, and his eyes fixed on mine he asked:

'Daddy, you don't think I'm mad do you?'

I was taken aback. I think I managed not to show it.

'Good heavens, no. What next? What on earth put such an idea into your head?'

'Well, it was Colin, really.'

'You haven't told him about Chocky?' I asked, with a quickening concern.

Matthew shook his head.

'Oh, no. I haven't told anyone but you, and Mummy – and Polly,' he added a little sadly.

'Good,' I approved. 'If I were you I'd keep it that way. But what about Colin?'

'I only asked him if he knew anyone who could hear someone talking kind of inside himself. I wanted to know,' he explained seriously. 'And he said no, because hearing voices was a well known first sign of madness, and people who did hear them either got put in asylums, or burnt at the stake, like Joan of Arc. So I sort of wondered ...'

'Oh, *that*,' I said, with more conviction than I was feeling.

'That's something quite different.' I searched hurriedly and desperately for a valid-sounding difference. 'He must have been thinking of the kind of voices that prophesy, tell of disasters to come, and try to persuade people to do foolish things so they get muddled over what's right and what's wrong, and what's sensible and what isn't. That's a different kind of voices altogether from ones that ask questions and tell about the binary code, and so on; quite different. He's probably only heard of the other kind, so he didn't understand what you meant. No, I should just forget it. You've no need to worry about that – no need at all.'

I must have sounded more convincing than I felt. Matthew relaxed, and nodded.

'Good,' he said, with satisfaction. 'I think I'd hate to go mad. You see, I don't feel at all mad.'

When I reported on our session to Mary I suppressed any reference to the last part of it. I felt it would simply add to her anxiety without getting us any further, so I concentrated on my inquiries into the Y and N business.

'This Chocky affair seems to get more baffling,' I confessed. 'One expects children to keep on making discoveries – well, hang it, that's what education's all about – but one also expects them to be pretty pleased with themselves for making them. There seems to me to be something psychologically unsound, if it isn't downright screwy, when all progress is attributed to a sort of familiar, instead of to self. It just isn't normal – And yet we've got to admit that his interests have widened. He's taking more notice of more things than he used to. And lately he's been gaining a – a sort of air of responsibility: had you noticed that? . . . I suppose the important question is whether once-removed approach is likely to do any harm – the man Trimble wasn't very happy about the results of it, was he?'

'Oh, that reminds me,' Mary put in, 'I had a note today from Miss Toach who takes him for geography. It's a bit confused, but I think it is meant to thank us for helping to stimulate his interest in the subject while at the same time suggesting tactfully that we shouldn't try to push him too much.'

'Oh,' I said. 'More Chocky?'

'I don't know, but I rather suspect he's been asking her the sort of awkward questions he asked me – about where Earth *is*, and so on.'

I thought it over for some moments.

'Suppose we were to change our strategy – hit out at Chocky a bit . . .?' I suggested.

Mary shook her head.

'No,' she told me. 'I don't think that's the way. She'd probably go underground – I mean, he'd lose confidence in us, and turn secretive. And that'd be worse really, wouldn't it?'

I rubbed my forehead.

'It's all very difficult. It doesn't seem wise to go on encouraging him; and it seems unwise to discourage him. So what do we do?'

Four

We were still trying to make up our minds the next Tuesday.

That was the day I stopped on the way home to take delivery of a new car. It was a station-wagon that I'd been hankering after for some time. Lots of room for everyone, and for a load of gear in the back as well. We all piled in, and took it out for a short experimental run before supper. I was pleased with the way it handled and thought I'd get to like it. The others were enthusiastic, and by the time we returned it was generally voted that the Gore family was entitled to tilt its chins a degree or two higher.

I left the car parked in front of the garage ready to take Mary and me to a friend's house later on, and went to write a letter while Mary got the supper.

About a quarter of an hour later came the sound of Matthew's raised voice. I couldn't catch what he was saying; it was a noise of half-choked, inarticulate protest. Looking out of the window I noticed that several passers-by had paused and were looking over the gate with expressions of uncertain amusement. I went out to investigate. I found Matthew standing a few feet from the car, very red in the face, and shouting incoherently. I walked towards him.

'What's the trouble, Matthew?' I inquired.

He turned. There were tears of childish rage running down his flushed cheeks. He tried to speak, but choked on the words, and grabbed my hand with both of his. I looked at the car which seemed to be the focus of the trouble. It did not appear damaged, nor to have anything visibly amiss with it. Then, conscious of the spectators at the gate, I led Matthew round to the other side of the house, out of their sight. There I sat down on one of the veranda chairs, and took him on my knee. I had never seen him so upset. He was shaking with anger, half-strangled by it, and still with tears copiously streaming. I put an arm round him.

'There now, old man. Take it easy. Take it easy,' I told him.

Gradually the shaking and the tears began to subside. He breathed more easily. By degrees the tension in him relaxed, and he grew quieter. After a time he heaved a great, exhausted sigh. I handed him my handkerchief. He plied it a bit, and then he blew.

'Sorry, Daddy,' he apologized through it, still chokily.

'That's all right, old man. Just take your time.'

Presently he lowered the handkerchief and plucked at it, still breathing jerkily. A few more tears, but of a different kind, overflowed. He cleaned up once more, sighed again, and began to be more like his normal self.

'Sorry, Daddy,' he said again. 'All right now – I think.'

'Good,' I told him. 'But dear, oh dear, what was all that about?'

Matthew hesitated, then he said,

'It was the car.'

I blinked.

'The car! For heaven's sake. It seems to be all right. What's it done to you?'

'Well, not the car, exactly,' Matthew amended. 'You see, it's a jolly nice car, I think it's super, and I thought Chocky would be interested in it, so I started showing it to her, and telling her how it works, and things.'

I became aware of a slight sinking, here-we-go-again feeling.

'But Chocky wasn't interested?' I inquired.

Something seemed to rise in Matthew's throat, but he

took himself in hand, swallowed hard and continued bravely:

'She said it was silly, and ugly, and clumsy. She – she *laughed* at it!'

At the recollection of this enormity his indignation swelled once more, and all but overwhelmed him. He strove to fight it down.

I was beginning to feel seriously worried. That the hypothetical Chocky could provoke such a near-hysterical condition of anger and outrage was alarming. I wished I knew more about the nature and manifestations of schizophrenia. However, one thing was clear, this was not the moment for debunking Chocky, on the other hand it was necessary to say something. I asked:

'What does she find so amusing about it?'

Matthew sniffed, paused, and sniffed again.

'Pretty nearly everything,' he told me, gloomily. 'She said the engine is funny, and old-fashioned, and wasteful, and that an engine that needed gears was ridiculous anyway. And that a car that didn't use an engine to stop itself as well as make itself go was stupid. And how it was terribly funny to think of anyone making a car that had to have springs because it just bumped along the ground on wheels that had to have things like sausages fastened round them.

'So I told her that's how cars are, anyway, and ours is a new car, and a jolly good one. And she said that was nonsense because our car is just silly, and nobody with any brains would make anything so clumsy and dangerous, and nobody with any sense would ride in one. And then – well, it's a bit muddled after that because I got angry. But, anyway, I don't care what *she* thinks: I *like* our new car.'

It was difficult. His indignation was authentic: a stranger would not have doubted for a moment that he had been engaged in a dispute which was not only genuine, but impassioned. Any lingering doubt I may have had as to whether we really needed advice about

Matthew was swept away then. However, rather than risk a wrong step now, I kept up the front.

'What does she think cars ought to be like, then?' I asked.

'That's what *I* asked her when she started on our car,' said Matthew. 'And she said that where she comes from the cars don't have wheels at all. They go along a bit above the ground, and they don't make any noise, either. She said that our kind of cars that have to keep to roads are bound to run into one another pretty often, and that, anyway, properly made cars are made so that they *can't* run into one another.'

'There's quite a lot to be said for that – if you can manage it,' I admitted. 'But, tell me, where *does* Chocky come from?'

Matthew frowned.

'That's one of the things we can't find out,' he said. 'It's too difficult. You see, if you don't know where anything else is, how can you find out where you are?'

'You mean, no reference points?' I suggested.

'I expect that's it,' Matthew said, a little vaguely. 'But I think where Chocky lives must be a very, very long way away. *Everything* seems to be different there.'

'H'm,' I said. I tried another tack. 'How old is Chocky?' I asked.

'Oh, pretty old,' Matthew told me. 'Her time doesn't go like ours though. But we worked it out that if it did she'd be at least twenty. Only she says she'll go on living until she's about two hundred, so that sort of makes twenty seem less. She thinks only living until you're seventy or eighty like we do, is silly and wasteful.'

'Chocky,' I suggested, 'appears to think a great many things silly.'

Matthew nodded emphatically.

'Oh, she does,' he agreed. 'Nearly everything, really,' he added, in amplification.

'Rather depressing,' I commented.

'It does get a bit boring pretty often,' Matthew conceded.

Then Mary called us in to supper.

I found myself increasingly at a loss to know what to do about it. Matthew had evidently had enough sense of self-protection not to tell any of his friends or school-fellows about Chocky. He had confided in Polly, possibly, I thought with some idea of sharing Chocky with her, but that had certainly been a failure. Yet, quite clearly, he found it a relief to talk about her – and after the car incident I had undoubtedly provided a very sorely needed safety-valve. Nevertheless, one had the feeling that at most times he was talking circumspectly – as if he were holding himself ready to bolt for cover at any unsympathetic response. The question seemed to be which of several possible courses was least likely to raise his defences.

Mary, when I told her about the car incident that evening, was inclined to favour the straightforward line of asking our regular doctor, Dr Aycott, to recommend a consultant. I was not. Not that I had anything against old Aycott. I wouldn't deny that the old boy was an adequate enough pill-pusher, but I couldn't help feeling that the Matthew problem was not in his line. Moreover, I pointed out, Matthew did not like him so it was improbable that he would confide in him. It seemed much more likely that he would consider we had abused his confidence by mentioning the matter to Aycott at all; in which case there was a risk that he would clam up altogether.

Mary, upon reflection, admitted the validity of that.

'But,' she said, 'It's getting to the point where we can't just go on letting it drift. We must *do* something. . . . And you can't simply pick a psychiatrist out of a list with a pin. You want the right kind of psychiatrist, proper recommendations, and all the rest of it . . .'

'I think I may have a line on that,' I told her. 'I was

telling Alan about it the other day, and he mentioned a man I used to know slightly at Cambridge; a fellow called Landis – Roy Landis. Alan knew him rather better, and he's kept in touch with him. It appears that after Landis qualified he went in for mental disorders. He's got a job at the Claudesley now, so he must be some good at it. Alan suggested it might be worth having a try at him – informally, just to give us a lead. If he were willing to have a look at Matthew he'd be able to tell us whether we ought to consult somebody professionally, and who would be the best man for the job. Or, possibly, it might be in his own line, and he'd take it on himself. We'd have to see.'

'Good,' Mary approved. 'You tackle him, then, and see if you can get him to come down. At least we shall feel that we're doing *something* . . .'

Time, and professional precept, can work wonders. I could scarcely recognize the rather untidy undergraduate I remembered in the well brushed, neatly bearded, elegant suited Roy Landis who joined Alan and me at the club for dinner, and I had to admit that these superficialities, plus a responsible manner, go a long way to establishing confidence. They are also somewhat intimidating. I had a slightly uneasy feeling of medical ethics lurking in ambush.

However, I plunged in. I stressed that our immediate need was advice upon the best steps to take, and told him something of Matthew. His professional caution relaxed as he listened, and his interest plainly grew. The episode with the new car particularly seemed to intrigue him. He asked a number of questions which I answered as best I could, beginning to feel hopeful. In the end he agreed to drive down to Hindmere the following Sunday week. He also gave me some instructions on preparing the ground for the visit, so that I was able to return home to report to Mary with a feeling of relief that, at last, we had things under way.

The next evening I told Matthew:

'I had dinner with an old friend of mine last night. I think you might like to meet him.'

'Oh,' said Matthew, not much interested in my old friends.

'The thing was,' I went on, 'we were talking cars, and he seems to have some of the same ideas as you told me Chocky has about them. He thinks our present cars are rather crude.'

'Oh,' said Matthew again. Then, with a steady look, he asked:

'Did you tell him about Chocky?'

'Well, I had to – a bit. You see, I could scarcely pretend that her ideas are yours, because they certainly aren't. He seemed interested, but not much surprised. Not nearly so surprised as I was when you first told me about Chocky. I rather got the idea he may have run across someone a bit like her before.'

Matthew showed signs of interest, but he was still cautious.

'Someone who talks to him the same way?' he inquired.

'No,' I admitted. 'Not to him, but to someone – or it may be more than one person – that he knows. Anyway, as I said, he didn't seem very surprised. I'm afraid we didn't go into it a great deal, but I thought you might like to know.'

That turned out to be a promising start. Matthew returned to the subject of his own accord a couple of times. Clearly, he was more than a little fascinated by the idea of someone who found Chocky unsurprising.

It was that, as well as the prospect of reassurance it held for him, I thought, that prompted him to admit that he might like to have a talk with Roy Landis, some-day.

The next Saturday we gave the new car its first real outing down to the coast. We bathed, and picnicked, and then Mary and I lazed in the sun while the children wandered off to amuse themselves.

Half-past five was packing-up time. Polly was easily found and separated from a gang of young acquaintances but there was no sign of Matthew. At six o'clock he was still missing. I decided to take a run along in the car to see if I could find him while Mary and Polly stayed where they were in case he should turn up.

I had got right down by the harbour before I spotted him. He was in earnest conversation with a policeman. I drew up nearby, and Matthew saw me.

'Oh, hullo Daddy,' he called. He glanced up at the policeman, and began to move towards the car. The policeman followed, and lifted his hand to his helmet.

'Good afternoon, sir,' he said. 'I've just been having to explain to your young man that it won't do.' He shook his head, and then added, by way of explanation: 'You can't expect people to put up with you going exploring on their boats, any more than they'd put up with you going exploring in their houses, can you now?'

'Certainly not Constable,' I agreed. 'Is that what you've been up to, Matthew?'

'I was just looking, Daddy. I didn't think anybody would mind. I wasn't *doing* anything.'

'But you were on the boat?'

'Yes, Daddy.'

It was my turn to shake my head.

'It's not the proper thing at all, Matthew. The Constable's quite right. I hope you've apologized.' I glanced at the policeman, and caught a slight flicker of his right eyelid.

'It's right he wasn't doing any harm there, sir,' the man agreed. 'But it's like you said, not at all a proper way to go on.'

Matthew looked up at the policeman.

'I'm sorry, sir,' he said. 'It's only that I never sort of thought of ships being like people's houses. I'll remember what you said.' And he held out his hand.

They shook, seriously.

'Come along now. We're late,' I said. 'Thank you very much, Constable.'

The policeman grinned, and raised his hand to his helmet again as we drove off.

'What *had* you been doing?' I inquired.

'What I said: just looking,' said Matthew.

'Well, you were lucky. I only hope I am as lucky with the next policeman I meet. An amiable man.'

'Yes,' said Matthew.

During the pause that followed he became aware that another apology was due.

'Sorry about being late, Daddy. I didn't notice the time.' As if he felt more explanation was needed he went on: 'You see Chocky's never seen a ship – not close to, I mean – so I was showing her. But a man put his head up through a hole, and got angry, and took me to the policeman.'

'Oh, I see. So it was really Chocky's fault?'

'Not really,' Matthew said, fairly. 'I mean, *I* thought she'd be interested.'

'H'm,' I said. 'It seems to me more likely that if she was running true to form she'd think ships are silly.'

'She does, rather,' Matthew admitted. 'She said it must waste an awful lot of power to keep on pushing all that water out of the way, and wouldn't it be more sensible, if you have to have ships, to build them to go just above the water and have only to push air out of the way.'

'Well, she's a bit late on that one. You tell her we have hovercraft already,' I suggested, as we arrived back at our bathing place and the waiting Mary and Polly.

During the following week I felt even more glad that Landis was coming down the next Sunday. For one thing Matthew's school report arrived. While, on the whole, it was not *un*satisfactory, I detected a slightly puzzled air about parts of it.

Mr Trimble acknowledged that Matthew had made progress – of a kind, but felt that he was capable of doing much better if he could confine his attention to the orthodox forms of mathematics.

Miss Toach, while she was glad to record that his interest in her subject had sharpened considerably, thought he would do better to concentrate on geography at present, and let cosmography come later.

Mr Caffer, the physics master, was not entirely pleased. He wrote: 'There has been a marked difference in his approach this term. If it were to show itself less in a capacity to ask questions, and more in ability to absorb information, his work would improve.'

'What have you been doing to Mr Caffer?' I asked.

'He gets annoyed,' said Matthew. 'There was one time when I wanted to know about the pressure of light, and another time when I told him I can see what gravity does, but I don't see *why* it does it. I don't think he knows why, and there were some other things, too. He wanted to know where I was getting the questions from. I couldn't very well tell him they came out of things Chocky had told me. So he got a bit riled. But it's all right now. I mean, it's not much good asking him things, so I haven't any more.'

'And there's Miss Blayde, biology. She seems to be a bit sniffy, too,' I said.

'Oh, I expect that's because I asked her how people who had only one sex managed to reproduce. She said, well, everybody had only one sex, and I said what I meant was one kind of person, all alike, not different like men and women. She said that could be in some plants, but not in people. And I said not always, and she said nonsense. But I said it wasn't nonsense because I happened to know someone like that. And she said what *did* I mean – in *that* kind of voice. Then I saw it had been dim of me to ask at all, because I couldn't tell her about Chocky, so I shut up, although she kept on wanting to know what I meant. And ever since then she sometimes looks at me very hard. That's all really.'

Miss Blayde was not the only one to feel baffled. A little time before, trying to get some idea what type of mental projection this Chocky was, I had asked:

'Doesn't Chocky have a home? Doesn't she even tell you about her mother and father, and where she lives – that kind of thing?'

'Not much,' said Matthew. 'I can't make out what it's like. You see, such a lot of the things she says don't mean anything.'

I said I was afraid I didn't quite see. Matthew had frowned in concentration.

'Well,' he said, 'suppose I was quite, quite deaf and you tried to tell me about a tune – I wouldn't be able to know what you were talking about, would I? It's a bit like that – sort of – I think. . . . She does sometimes talk about her father, or her mother – but the hims and hers get mixed up, as if they were both the same.'

I wondered what complex we were on the brink of now, and tried to recall the name of some suitably gynandrous Greek, but it eluded me. I said merely that it must be confusing. Matthew agreed.

'But our way is difficult for her to understand, too,' he told me. '*She* thinks it must be terribly confusing to have *two* parents, and not a good idea at all. She says it is natural and easy to love one person, but if your parent is divided into two different people it must be pretty difficult for your mind not to be upset by trying not to love one more than the other. She thinks it's very likely the strain of that which accounts for some of the peculiar things about us.'

This reportage of Chocky's ideas gave me some sympathy with Miss Blayde's bewilderment. It also made me thankful that I had already approached Landis – though, at the same time my anxiety over his verdict was somewhat sharpened.

The next thing was that Mary's sister Janet rang up and gave her usual short notice of intention to pay us a visit over the week-end. Mary explained that we were engaged on Sunday, and fended off inquiries as to the exact nature of the engagement.

'Oh, well, too bad, but never mind,' said Janet, 'we can easily make it Friday, and leave on Sunday directly after breakfast. It'll give us a chance of seeing more of the country on the way home.'

'Damn,' said Mary as she hung up. 'The trouble with Janet is that when she makes up her mind it just scatters my wits. Why on earth didn't I put her off till the next week-end? Oh, well, too late now.'

Five

On Friday evening Janet and her husband, Kenneth, arrived, accompanied by their two youngest. They showed up, true to form, an hour and a half later than the time she had given, and thereafter for twenty-four hours the visit grooved along its usual pattern. Mary and Janet discussed Janet's children, their sister Patience's children, brothers Ted's and Frank's children, and those of a number of mutual friends. Kenneth and I kept mostly to the safe, and only slightly controversial, topic of cars. Altogether it went quite smoothly. It was only on Saturday evening that Janet, apparently realizing that in all their conversations about children they had missed out Mary's, decided to remedy the omission.

'Of course it's none of my business,' she said, 'but I always think that a fresh eye sometimes sees perhaps a little more than one that's always there, don't you?'

One recognized the gambit. I glanced at Mary. Her attention was all on her knitting.

'It could be. On the other hand, it has had less chance to observe,' she replied.

Janet's question had been rhetorical. She was not to be deflected by generalizations. She went on:

'It struck me that Matthew is looking a wee bit peaky – just a bit off colour, perhaps?'

'Indeed?' said Mary.

'You've not noticed it? That's what I meant. Perhaps he's been overworking a bit – they often outgrow their strength at his age, don't they?'

'Really?' said Mary.

'Or perhaps he isn't strong naturally,' Janet suggested.

Mary had finished her row. She laid the knitting on her knee, and smoothed it over.

'He seems quite strong and healthy to us,' she said. 'Doesn't he, David?'

I picked up my cue.

'Certainly he does,' I put in. 'Never anything more than the odd cold – and I don't know how you stop any child catching that,' I backed her up.

'I'm so glad to hear that,' Janet said. 'Still one can't be too watchful. After all, it's not as if we knew a great deal about his hereditary tendencies, is it? Doesn't he strike you as being a bit listless sometimes – a little introverted, perhaps?'

'I don't think he does,' Mary told her.

'Ah, that's what I meant about the fresh eye. He does to me. And my Tim tells me he talks to himself a lot.'

'Many children think out loud.'

'Of course, but according to my Tim he often says some rather odd things, too. There is such a thing as a child having too much imagination, you know.'

Mary paused in her knitting.

'What kind of odd things?' she asked.

'Tim doesn't remember, really, but they seemed to him distinctly – well, odd.'

I felt it was time I took a hand.

'Yes,' I said, 'I can understand that. Matthew is perhaps a trifle too sensitive. Your Tim is so unmistakably a healthy extravert type. Mens stulta in corpore sano, and all that.'

Janet heard what she expected to hear.

'Exactly,' she agreed. 'And that, of course, makes one so conscious of the difference between them.'

'It's bound to,' I agreed. 'Your Tim is so splendidly normal. It's hard to imagine him saying anything odd. Though I sometimes think,' I went on, 'that it's a pity that thorough normality is scarcely achievable except at some cost to individuality. Still, there it is, that's what normality means – average.'

'Oh, I wouldn't call Tim average exactly,' Janet protested, and went on to explain, with instances, why Tim was not. The subject of Matthew somehow got lost in the exposition, and was not revived.

'I'm glad you headed her off,' Mary said, when we got upstairs. 'Though you were a bit hard on her Tim. He's not all that dull.'

'Of course he isn't, but your sister, darling, is an inquisitive, and, I'm afraid, not very intelligent, woman. Like all parents she is dichotomous, what she really wants is a child genius who is perfectly normal. She hinted that Matthew isn't quite normal, and put us on the defensive. So I hinted that Tim, while perfectly normal, isn't very bright. So she promptly went over to the defensive. Elementary, my dear.'

'All the same, she was right about one thing. We *don't* know anything of Matthew's heredity, do we?'

'And we certainly don't know that his heredity has anything to do with this Chocky business, so let's just wait and see what Landis has to tell us tomorrow.'

Janet and her lot were, inevitably, late in getting under way, but we managed to wave them off at last about twenty minutes before Landis's car slid into our drive. He arrived, as becomes a with-it medical man, in a large, well-groomed Jaguar.

I made the introductions. Mary appeared a little reserved, but Matthew, I was glad to see, seemed to take to him easily. After lunch we all adjourned to the veranda for a quarter of an hour or so, then, by arrangement, Mary took Polly off with her, I mentioned some work I must do, and Matthew and Landis were left alone together.

Tea time came, and I looked out to find Matthew still talking hard. Landis caught my eye, and decisively frowned me away.

The three of us decided not to wait, which was just as

well, for it was nearly six o'clock before the other two broke up their conclave and joined us. They appeared to be on excellent terms. Matthew in rather better spirits, I thought, than he had been lately; Landis, inclined to be quietly reflective.

We let the children have their supper first, and get along to bed. Then, when we sat down to our meal there was a chance to talk. Mary opened up with:

'Well, you two certainly did have a session. I do hope Matthew wasn't too tedious.'

Landis regarded her for a moment, and shook his head.

'Tedious!' he repeated. 'Oh, no. I assure you he wasn't that.' He turned to me. 'You know, you didn't tell me the half of it,' he said, with a touch of reproof.

'I don't suppose I know half of it,' I replied. 'I told you most of what I do know, but to find out more I'd have had to press him for it. I thought that might be un-wise – I'm not so old as to have forgotten how intrusive one's parents' interest can seem. That's why I asked you to come. Quite apart from your professional experience, I hoped he'd feel freer to talk to you. Apparently he did.'

'He did indeed,' Landis nodded. 'Yes, I think you probably were wise not to push him – though it meant that I felt a bit ill-briefed to start with. I found him more puzzled, and more in need of someone to talk to about it than you had led me to expect. However, he's got a lot of it off his chest now, and I think he'll be feeling the better for that, at least.'

He paused a moment, and then turned to Mary.

'Tell me, Mrs Gore, normally – that is to say before this Chocky business set in – would you have called him a highly imaginative boy?'

Mary considered.

'I don't think so,' she said. 'As a little boy, he was very *suggestible*. I mean, we always had to get him safely out of the room before anyone turned on a tap – but that's not quite the same thing, is it? No, I'd not say he was *highly* imaginative – just ordinarily.'

Landis nodded.

'An open mind is a difficult thing to keep. I must admit that from what David told me I rather suspected he might be an imaginative child who had been reading too much fantastic stuff – to a point where he was having difficulty in distinguishing it from reality. That set me on the wrong track . . .'

'He must have read some. They all do,' I put in, 'but his taste in fiction really runs more to simple adventure stories – "Biggles", and so on.'

'Yes, I got on to that fairly soon. So I changed my line of thought . . . and then had to change it again.'

For quite a long pause he toyed with the cold meat on his plate until Mary became impatient.

'But what do you think it is now?' she asked.

Landis delayed another moment or two before he looked up. When he did so, he stared at the opposite wall with a curiously far away expression.

'After all,' he said 'you are not consulting me professionally. If you were, I would say it is a complex case needing more than a short examination can reveal: I would stall. But I am going to be unprofessional. I am going to confess that I don't know: it has me beat . . .'

He broke off, and fiddled with his knife. Mary's eyes met mine. We said nothing.

'I don't understand it,' Landis repeated. 'I know what it *looks* like – but that's sheer nonsense . . .'

He broke off again.

'What does it look like?' I prompted, a little sharply.

He hesitated, and then drew a breath.

'More than anything I've ever come across it resembles what our unscientific ancestors used to consider a case of "possession". They would have claimed quite simply that this Chocky is a wandering, if not a wanton, spirit which has invaded Matthew.'

There was a silence. I broke it.

57

'But that being, as you said, nonsense . . .?'

'I don't know. . . . One must be careful not to be as dogmatic in our way as our ancestors were in theirs. It's easy to over-simplify – that is just what Matthew himself is doing when he says he "talks to", or is "talked to", by this Chocky. The ancestors would say he "hears voices", but that is only a manner of speaking. Matthew only uses the word "talks" because he has no word for what he really means. When he "listens" to Chocky there are no words: he is not really hearing sounds at all. When he replies he doesn't *need* to use words – he sometimes does, particularly when he is feeling worked up, but he does it because it is his natural way of expressing his emotions, not because it is necessary. Therefore his "hearing" a voice is a metaphorical expression – *but* the conversations he holds with this imagined voice are *not* metaphorical. They are quite real.'

Mary was frowning.

'You'll have to explain that more,' she said.

'Well, for one thing, it is quite indisputable that there is some kind of sound intelligence somehow involved,' Landis said. 'Just think back to some of the questions he has been asking, and the things he has said to you and David. We're satisfied he did not invent them himself; that's why I am here at all, but wasn't it characteristic of all of them that they were naïvely, sometimes childishly expressed?'

'After all, he's not quite twelve,' Mary pointed out.

'Exactly, and in fact he has an unusually good vocabulary, for a child of his age – but it isn't adequate to express clearly the questions he wants to ask. He *knows* what he wants to ask, and often understands quite well what he wants to tell. His chief difficulty is in finding the words to make the ideas clear.

'Now if he were passing on questions he had heard, he wouldn't have that particular difficulty. He'd simply repeat the words, whether he had understood them, or not. Or if he'd read the questions in a book he'd know the words. In either case he'd be using the words he needs instead of having this trouble with the limits of his vocabulary.

'It follows, therefore, that he did not, in the ordinary sense, *hear* these questions, nor read them; yet he does understand what he is trying to ask. So – how did the questions get into his head without the words necessary to carry them there? – And that really is quite a problem . . .'

'But is it – any more than it always is?' Mary said. 'Words are only names for ideas. Everybody gets ideas. They have to come into minds from somewhere before they can be given names.'

I knew the pitch of her voice. Something – possibly, I suspected Landis's use of the word 'possession' – had made her antagonistic.

Landis went on:

'Take his use of the binary code. If anyone had shown him, or if he had seen it in a book, the odds are that the symbols used would have been nought and one, or plus and minus, or possibly x and y, and he would naturally have used the same symbols himself. But the way he did get them appeared to him simply as an affirmative and a negative, so he conveniently abbreviated them to Y and N.'

'But,' Mary objected, 'if, as you say, there aren't any words so that he isn't listening when he seems to be, what is going on? I mean, why this idea of this Chocky who "talks" at all?'

'Oh, Chocky exists all right. Naturally, I looked at first for some personification of his subconscious, however I was sure quite soon that it wasn't that. But where Chocky exists, and what she is, beats me completely at present – and it beats Matthew, too.'

That was not what Mary had hoped to hear. She said: 'I can understand that *for him* she exists. She's quite real *to him*: that's why we've been playing up to it, but . . .'

Landis cut her short:

'Oh, Chocky has a much more definite existence than that. I am quite satisfied that whatever she is, she is more than his own invention.'

'His *conscious* invention,' I qualified, 'but might she not be the product of a complex?'

I wished I could name that gynandrous Greek: surely they could not have missed a thing like *that* out of their mythology, but it still eluded me.

Landis shook his head.

'I don't think so. Considered as a projection of his own subconscious she isn't viable. I'll tell you why. Consider the car incident. Now, no boy of Matthew's age would dream for a moment of calling a brand new model of a modern car old-fashioned. He thinks it's wonderful. Matthew himself was proud of it, and anxious to show it off. But, according to your account, what happened was exactly what would have happened if another child – or anyone else, for that matter – had been scornful of it – except that no other child, nor his own subconscious, would have been able to explain how it ought to be radically different.

'And here's another one he told me this afternoon. He was, he said, explaining to Chocky about the use of step-rockets for space-flight. She laughed at the idea, just as she had at the car. According to him she thought it ludicrous, and old – I think he meant primitive. Weight, she told him, is a force, and a force is a form of energy: it is both costly and foolish to oppose one form of energy directly to another. First one should study to understand the nature of the hindering force. Once it is properly understood, one is able to discover the way to negate it, if not the way to make it work *for* instead of against one. Thus, the proper way to operate a space-ship is not to attempt to smash it into the sky with explosives against the whole pull of gravitation, but to develop a means of screening-off that pull.

'In this way, she explained, by balancing the reduced pull against the centrifugal force, you achieve a smooth take-off and a steady rate of acceleration. A reasonably supportable rate of acceleration giving only two or three Gs soon builds up to a far greater speed than any rocket could ever attain, without causing any distress. By manipulating the gravity-screens you can determine your direction, and increase or decrease your speed as you wish.

'Rocketry, she told Matthew, was simple (I think he meant naïve) like powering a car by clockwork, or petrol – once you've used up your stored power, you're finished: but with. ... And this is the point where we came unstuck – Matthew couldn't get the concept. It was a kind of power. It seemed to him something like electricity, but he knew that it was really quite different. ... Anyway, with this source of energy which can be picked up from space radiations and converted to operate motors or gravity-screens, there is no question of running out of power. The limit of speed which you can reach eventually is that of light. But you still have two obstacles to efficient space-travel. One is the altogether excessive time taken by acceleration and deceleration, and shortening this by increasing the Gs can only give too slight an improvement to bother with – and that at the cost of exhausting strain. The other, more funda-mental, trouble is that the speed of light is far too slow to allow one to attempt to cover the vast interstellar dis-tances. Somehow a way round that difficulty has to be found, the present most hopeful theory is – but there Matthew lost her again, among ideas that were quite beyond his grasp. As he put it to me: "She kept on going on, but it didn't mean anything. It wouldn't turn into proper words".'

Landis paused. Then he added:

'Now, that again, I'm quite satisfied, did not come out of books. It *could* have done, but it didn't. If it had, he would not have stumbled as he did in trying to find words to express what was quite clear in his mind.'

'I must say it's far from clear in my mind. How did all

that about space-ships get into it at all?' Mary asked him.

'Simply as an illustration. He has somehow been told that space-ships are inefficient, just as he was told that cars are inefficient.'

'And all that stuff seemed quite sensible to you – I mean, you feel that it *makes* sense?'

'Let's say that as far as it keeps within the bounds of his understanding, it is logical. One would rather it were not.'

'Why?' Mary demanded.

'Because if there had been some slips caused by mis-understandings, or by embroideries of his own which did not fit in with the rest, there'd still be the chance that he's concocted it out of things he's read. As it is, he freely ad-mits he couldn't understand a lot of it, and it appears that for the rest he's doing an honest job of reporting. It would be a lot simpler if one could believe that, even subcon-sciously, he had compiled the whole thing for himself.

'And there were other things, too. Apparently, accord-ing to Chocky, we, in our civilization, are still suffering from a primitive fixation on the wheel. Once we had dis-covered rotary motion we applied it to everything; only recently are our inventions beginning to show signs of breaking free from the wheel-obsession. Now, where would a boy pick up an idea like that?'

'Very well,' I said, 'suppose we agree that subcon-scious promptings are to be ruled out. What's to be done about it?'

Landis shook his head again.

'At present I've, quite frankly, no idea. At the moment I can't see – quite unscientifically can't see – anything for it but to take a catch-phrase literally – I don't know what's got into him. I wish I did. Something has.'

Mary got up from the table abruptly and decisively. We loaded the dishes on to the trolley, and she pushed it out. A few minutes later she came back with coffee. As she poured it out she said to Landis:

'So what it amounts to is that all you have to tell us

is that you can't see any way of helping Matthew, is that it?'

Landis's brow furrowed.

'Helping him?' he repeated. 'I don't know. I'm not even sure that he needs help. His chief need at the moment seems to be for someone he can talk to about this Chocky. He doesn't particularly like her, in fact she frequently irritates him, but she does supply him with a great deal that interests him. In fact, it doesn't seem to be so much Chocky's existence that troubles him, as his own self-defensive instinct to keep her existence hidden – and in that he's wise. Until now you two have been his only safety-valves. His sister might have been another, but she appears to have let him down.'

Mary stirred her coffee, gazing at its vortex with abstraction. Then, making up her mind, she said, forthrightly:

'Now *you're* talking as if this Chocky really exists. Let's get this straight. Chocky is a convention of Matthew's. It is simply a name for an imagined companion – just as Polly's Piff was. One quite understands that that is not unusual, and nothing to worry about – up to a point. But carried beyond that point it *is* something to worry about because it has ceased to be normal. Very well, then, it has seemed to us for some little time now that Matthew has passed that point. Something *ab*normal has happened to him. It is because of that that David appealed to you for advice.'

Landis considered her for a moment before he replied:

'I'm afraid I can't have made myself clear,' he said. 'Any resemblance between Chocky and Piff is quite superficial. I would like to believe what you wish to believe – and what my training tells me I should believe – that the whole thing is subjective. That Chocky is a child's invention, like Piff – an invention of Matthew's own which has got out of hand. But I can only do that by ignoring the evidence. Well, I'm not bigoted enough to twist the facts to suit what I have been taught;

Chocky is, in some way I don't understand, objective – she comes from outside, not from inside. On the other hand I'm not credulous enough to accept the old idea of "possession", although it fits the evidence much better . . .' He broke off in thought for some seconds, and then shook his head:

'No. That's not so, either. "Possession" meant what it said: domination. This is not. It is much more like a working arrangement . . .'

'What on earth do you mean by that?' Mary demanded.

The sharpness of her voice told me that any confidence she may have had in Landis had ebbed away entirely. Landis himself appeared not to notice it. His reply was unruffled:

'You will remember that when he was ill he told Chocky to shut up and go away – which, with your added persuasion she apparently did. She seems to have done the same after she had reduced him to speechless anger over the car. *He* rejected *her*. She does not dominate . . .

'I asked him about that. He told me that when she first started to "talk" to him she would do it at any time. It might be when he was in class, or doing his homework, or at mealtimes, or, quite often at night. He didn't like his work, or his own interests being arbitrarily interrupted; he did not like it when there were other people present – it made them look at him oddly because he could not pay attention to her and to others at the same time; and, still more, he disliked being woken up in the middle of the night with impossible questions.

'So, he tells me, he simply refused to cooperate unless she would come only at times when he could give her his full attention. And that, incidentally, seems to have given them some trouble because, he said: "Chocky's time isn't the same sort of time as ours", and he had to get round that by setting the kitchen timer to demonstrate the exact duration of an hour. Once they had that established, she had a scale, and they could arrange for her to come at times when he was not busy – times to suit him not her, you notice ...

'And notice, too, how practical this was. No element of fantasy at all. Simply a boy laying it down that his friend should visit him only at convenient times. And the friend apparently willing to accept the conditions he offered.'

Mary was not impressed. Indeed, I was doubtful whether she listened. She said impatiently:

'I don't understand this. When the Chocky business began David and I thought it would be unwise to try to suppress it. We assumed that it would soon pass. We were wrong: it seemed to take a firmer hold. I became uneasy. One doesn't have to be a psychologist to know the result of a fantasy gaining the same validity as reality. I agreed to David asking you to come because I thought you would suggest some course we could take which would rid Matthew of his fantasy without harming him. Instead, you seem to have spent the day encouraging him in it – and to have become infected with it yourself. I am not able to feel that this is doing much good to Matthew, or to anyone.'

Landis looked as if he were about to make a sharp answer, but he checked the impulse.

'The first requirement,' he said, 'is to understand the condition. In order to do that it is necessary to gain his confidence.'

'This is quite obvious,' Mary told him, 'and I understand perfectly well that while you were with Matthew it was necessary for you to seem to accept the reality of this Chocky – we've been doing the same for weeks. What I do not understand is why you keep it up when Matthew is no longer here.'

Landis asked patiently:

'But, Mrs Gore, consider the questions he has been putting, and the things he has been saying. Don't they seem to you odd – intelligently odd – but quite out of his usual key?'

'Of course they do,' she replied sharply. 'But boys read all kinds of things: one expects it. And it's no surprise that what they pick up makes them ask questions. What is disturbing us is the way he twists all his natural curiosity into support for this Chocky fantasy. Can't you see, I'm afraid of it becoming a permanent obsession? What I want to know is simply the best way of stopping that from happening.'

Landis attempted once more to explain why, in his view, Chocky could not be considered as a simple fantasy, but Mary had now worked herself into a mood where she obstinately refused to accept any of his points. I wished very strongly that he had not made that ill-advised reference to 'possession'. It seemed to me an error of judgement – of a kind one did not expect from a psychologist – and once it had been made the damage was done.

There was nothing for me to do but sit by and watch them consolidate their opposition.

It was a relief to all of us when Landis at last decided to give it up, and leave.

Six

I found the situation awkward. I could follow Landis's reasoning – though I would be hanged if I could see where it was leading him – but I had also some sympathy for Mary's impatience. Landis, however unseriously he may have intended it, had, for a psychiatrist, made a bad psychological error. It would have been better, in my opinion, for him not to have referred to ancient beliefs at all; particularly, he should not have used the word 'possession'. There are fears that we would strongly assert, and honestly believe, we have outgrown which, nevertheless, still lie dormant in all of us, ready to be aroused by a careless, unexpected word used at a critical moment. All the visit seemed to have done was to add an element of irrationality to Mary's anxiety. Moreover, as much as what he said, his unhurried, detached, analytical attitude to the problem had irritated her. Her concern was immediate. There was something wrong with Matthew, and she wanted it put right without delay. She had looked to Landis for advice on how that could best be done: what she had got was a dissertation on an interesting case, the more disquieting because of his admission that it baffled him. By the time he left she had been giving an impression of regarding him as little better than a charlatan. An unfortunate, and unfruitful occasion.

When I got home the following evening she had an abstracted air. After we had cleared the table and packed the children off upstairs there was an atmosphere that I recognized. Some kind of prepared statement, a little uncertain of its reception, was on its way. Mary sat down, a little more upright than usual, and addressed herself to the empty grate rather than to me. With a slightly challenging manner she announced:

'I went to see Dr Aycott today.'

'Oh,' I said. 'Something wrong?'

'About Matthew,' she added.

I looked at her.

'You didn't take Matthew to him?'

'No.' She shook her head. 'I thought of doing that, but decided against it.'

'I'm glad,' I told her. 'I rather think Matthew would have regarded that as a breach of confidence. It might be better if he doesn't know.'

'Yes,' she agreed, rather definitely.

'As I've said before,' I remarked, 'I've nothing against Aycott as a cut-stitcher and measles-spotter, but I don't feel this kind of thing is up his street.'

'You're right. It certainly isn't,' Mary agreed. She went on: 'Mind you, I didn't really expect that it would be. I did my best to tell him how things are. He listened not very patiently, and seemed a bit piqued that I hadn't brought Matthew himself along. I tried to explain to the old fool that I wasn't asking for an opinion then and there; all I wanted was a recommendation to a suitable specialist.'

'From which I gather that what you got was an opinion?'

She nodded, with a wry expression.

'Oh, yes indeed. All Matthew needs is plenty of exercise, a cold bath in the morning, plenty of good plain unseasoned food, lots of salads, and the window open at night,' she told me, with some tartness.

'And no specialist?'

'No. No need for that. Growing is often more exacting than we realize, but a healthy life, and Nature, the great healer, will soon correct any temporary imbalances.'

'I'm sorry,' I said.

There was a pause. It was Mary who broke it:

'David we must help him somehow.'

'Darling, I know you didn't take to Landis, but he is quite highly thought of, you know. He wouldn't say he's doubtful whether Matthew really needs help if he didn't mean it. We're both worried, but simply because we don't understand: we've really no warrant to assume that because this thing is unusual it is therefore harmful. I feel quite sure that if Landis had seen cause for alarm he'd have told us so.'

'I don't suppose he felt any. Matthew isn't his boy. He's just an unusual, rather puzzling case: quite interesting now, but if he were to become normal again he'd no longer be interesting.'

'Darling, that's a dreadful thing to imply. Besides, you know, Matthew isn't *ab*normal: he's perfectly normal, but plus something – which is quite different.'

Mary gave me the look she keeps for hair-splitting, and some other forms of tiresomeness.

'But it *is* different,' I insisted. 'There is an essential distinction . . .'

She cut that short ruthlessly.

'I don't care about that,' she said. 'All I want is for him to be normally normal, not plus or minus anything. I just want him to be happy.'

I decided to leave it there, for the time being. Except for his occasional bouts of frustration – and what child doesn't have those, one way or another? – Matthew did not seem to me to be *un*happy. But to say so then would have led us into an argument on the nature of happiness – a singularly inappropriate ground for battle.

The question of what was to be done remained, however. For my part, I favoured further contact with Landis: Matthew clearly felt able to confide in him, and he was undoubtedly interested by Matthew. But, with Mary turned against Landis, such a course would be in direct opposition to her wishes – only a highly critical situation could justify taking that. . . . And crisis and urgency were qualities that the Chocky affair appeared to lack . . .

So, for the present, as on several previous occasions, we

attempted to console ourselves with recollection of the
way in which Polly had suddenly expelled Piff from the
family.

In the meantime, however, I did suggest to Matthew
that as Mummy did not seem to care a lot for Chocky,
it might not be a bad idea to keep her rather in the background for a bit . . .

We heard very little of Chocky for about a fortnight
after that. Indeed, I began to have hopes that she was
leaving us; not, unfortunately, by summary dismissal,
which would have been satisfactorily definite, but by
something more like a slow fade-out. But they were only
slender hopes, and soon to be nipped.

One evening as I was reaching for the television switch
Mary stopped me. 'Just a minute,' she said. She got up
and went across to her bureau. When she came back she
was holding several sheets of paper, the largest about sixteen inches by twelve. She handed them to me without
a word, and went back to her chair.

I looked at the papers. Some of the smaller ones were
pencil sketches, the larger ones were paintings in poster-
colour. Rather odd paintings. The first two were landscapes, with a few figures. The scenes were undoubtedly
local, and vaguely familiar, though I could not positively
identify the viewpoints. The first thing that struck me
was the figures, they were treated with an individuality
of style that was quite constant: cows, and sheep, too, had
a rectangular and lean look; human beings appeared as a
half-way compromise between the real thing and stick-
men, noticeably lacking in bulk and surprisingly angular.
But despite that there was life and movement in them.

The drawing was firm and confident, the colouring
somewhat sombre; it gave an impression of being much
concerned with subtle shades of green. I know next to
nothing of painting, but they gave me a feeling that the
sureness of line, and the economy with which effects had
been achieved showed considerable accomplishment.

The next two were still-lifes: a vase of flowers, not seen as a botanist or a horticulturalist would see them, but, nevertheless, recognizably roses; and a bowl of red things, which, once one had made allowance for over-emphasis on the seeds, were undoubtedly strawberries.

Following these came a view through a window. This I was able to recognize. It showed a corner of a school playground, with a number of figures there that were active, but, again, spindly.

Then there were a couple of portraits. One of a man with a long rather severely-planed face. I – well, I cannot say I recognized it, but there was something about the hairline which seemed to imply that it was intended for myself – though to my mind my eyes do not in the least resemble traffic go-lights. The other portrait was of a woman; not Mary, nor anyone I could identify.

After I had studied the pictures I laid them down on my knees, and looked across at Mary. She simply nodded.

'You understand this kind of thing better than I do. Would you call them good?' I asked.

'I think so. They're odd, but there's life and movement in them, perception, a feeling of confidence. . . .' She let it tail away. Then added: 'It was accidental. I was clearing his room. They'd fallen behind the chest of drawers . . .'

I looked down at the top one again, at the emaciated cattle, and the spidery farmhand who wielded a pitchfork.

'Perhaps one of the children in his class – or his art-teacher . . . ?' I ventured.

Mary shook her head.

'Those aren't hers. I've seen some of Miss Soames' stuff: her style's a bit on the niggly side. Besides, the last one *is* her – not very flattering, either.'

I looked through the pictures once more, reconsidering them. They grew on one, once the first strangeness had worn off.

'You could put them back there tomorrow, and just say nothing,' I suggested.

Mary smoothed her knitting, and pulled it to get the rows straight.

'I could . . . but they'd go on worrying me. I'd rather he told us about them . . .'

I looked at the second landscape, and suddenly recognized the scene, knew the exact bend in the river which gave it.

'Darling,' I said, 'I'm afraid you won't like it.'

'I've not liked any of it. I didn't like it even before that friend of yours started talking about "possession". But I'd rather know than be left guessing. After all, it is just possible that someone did give them to him.'

Her expression told me that she meant what she said. I did not demur further, but it was with a feeling that the whole thing was now entering upon a new phase that I agreed. I took her hand, and pressed it.

'All right,' I said. 'He'll scarcely be in bed yet.' And I put my head into the hall, and called upstairs. Then I spread the pictures out on the floor.

Matthew arrived in his dressing-gown, pink, tousle-headed, and fresh from the bath. He stopped abruptly at the sight of the pictures. Then his eyes went to Mary's face, uneasily.

'I say, Matthew,' I said, as chattily as I could, 'Mummy happened to come across these when she was clearing your room. They'd slipped down behind the chest of drawers.'

'Oh,' said Matthew. '*That's* where they went.'

'They're very interesting, and we think they're rather good. Are they yours?'

Matthew hesitated, then:

'Yes,' he said, a little too defiantly.

'What I mean is,' I explained, 'did you paint them?'

This time his 'yes' had a defensive touch.

'H'm. . . . They aren't much like your usual style, are they? I should have thought you'd got higher marks for these than you usually do in Art,' I suggested.

Matthew shuffled a little.

'These ones aren't Art. They're private,' he told me.

I looked at one of the landscapes again.

'You seem to be seeing things in quite a different way,' I remarked.

'Yes,' Matthew agreed. Hopefully he added: 'I expect it's something to do with growing up.'

His eyes pleaded with me. After all, it was I who had advised him to be discreet.

'It's quite all right, Matthew. We're only interested to know who really did do them.'

Matthew hesitated. He darted an unhappy glance at Mary, looked down at the carpet in front of him, and traced one of the patterns there with his toe.

'*I* did,' he told us, but then his resolution appeared to weaken. He qualified: 'I mean – sort of – well, I *did* do them . . .'

He looked so miserable and confused that I was reluctant to press him further. It was Mary who came to his rescue. She put an arm round him.

'It doesn't really matter a bit, darling. It's just that we were so interested in them, we wanted to know.' She reached down and picked up a painting. 'This view. It's very clever. I think it's very good – but it's rather strange. Did it really look like that to you?'

Matthew stayed dumb for some seconds, then half-blurting he told her.

'I *did* do them, Mummy, really I did. Why they look sort of funny is because that's how Chocky sees things.'

He turned an anxious look on her, but Mary's face showed only interest.

'Tell us about it, darling,' she encouraged him.

Matthew looked relieved. He sighed.

'It happened one day after Art,' he explained. 'I don't seem to be much good at Art,' he added, regretfully. 'Miss Soames said what I had done was hopeless. And Chocky thought it was pretty bad, too. So I said I did try, but it never seemed to come out at all right, and Chocky said that was because I didn't look at things properly. So I said I didn't see where "properly" came into it; you either see things, or you don't. And she said no, it wasn't like that because you can look at things without seeing them, if you don't do it properly. And we argued a bit about that because it didn't seem sense.

'So in the end she said what about trying an experiment – me doing the drawing, and her doing the seeing? I didn't see how that could work, but she said she thought it was worth trying. So we did.

'It didn't come off the first few times because I couldn't think of nothing. The first time you try it's awfully hard to think of nothing. You sort of keep on thinking of not thinking of anything, but that isn't the same at all, so it doesn't work. But that's what Chocky said: just sit and hold a pencil and think of nothing. I got pretty fed up with trying, but she kept on wanting to have another go at it. And, well, about the fourth time we tried I half-managed it for a minute or two. After that it got easier, and then when we'd practised a bit more it got quite easy. So now I've only got to sit down with the paints and – well, sort of switch-off me, and the picture comes – only the way it comes is the way Chocky sees it, not the way I do.'

I could see Mary's fingers fidgeting, but her mask of impersonal interest remained unaltered. I said:

'I think I understand what you mean, Matthew. You sort of hand over to Chocky. But I should think that feels a bit funny, doesn't it?'

'Only the first time or two. Then I felt a bit like – well, no brakes. But after that it gets more like . . .' He paused for some moments searching with furrowed brow for a simile. His expression cleared slightly, '. . . it gets more like riding a bicycle, no hands.' He frowned again, and amended: 'Only not quite, because it's Chocky doing the steering, not me – sort of difficult to explain,' he added apologetically.

I could appreciate that it would be. More to give Mary

some reassurance than on my own account I asked:

'I suppose it doesn't ever happen when you don't want it to? By accident, I mean?'

Matthew shook his head emphatically.

'Oh no. I have to *make* it happen by thinking of nothing. Only now I don't have to keep on thinking of nothing all the time it's happening. The last few times I could watch my hands doing the pictures – so all the real doing them is mine. It's just the seeing what to do that isn't.'

'Yes, dear,' Mary said. 'We understand that, but . . .' she hesitated, searching for a gentle way to make her point, '. . . but do you think it is a good thing to do?'

Matthew glanced at the pictures.

'I think so, Mummy. They're much better pictures than I do, when they're all mine – even if they do look a bit funny,' he admitted candidly.

'That wasn't quite what I . . .' Mary began. Then she changed her mind, and looked at the clock.

'It's getting late,' she said, with a glance at me.

'That's right. It is,' I backed her up. 'But just before you go, Matthew, have you shown these to anyone else?'

'Well, not really *shown*,' he said. 'Miss Soames came in one day, just after I'd done that one.' He pointed to the view of the play-ground through the window. 'She said whose was it, which was a bit awkward because I couldn't pretend it was anyone else's, so I had to say it was mine, and she *looked* at me, the way people do when they don't believe you. Then she looked at the picture, and then back again at me. "All right", she said, "let's see you do a – a racing car, at speed". So then I had to explain that I couldn't do things that I couldn't see – I meant that Chocky couldn't see for me, but I couldn't tell her that. And she looked at me hard again, and said: "Very well, what about the view through the other window?"

'So I turned the easel round, and did that. She took it off the board and stared at it for a long time, then she looked at me very queerly, and said did I mind if she kept it? I couldn't very well say I did, so I said no, and, please, could I go now? And she nodded, and went on staring at it.'

'It's funny she said nothing about it in your report,' I told him.

'Oh, it was right at the end of term; after reports,' he explained.

I felt a premonitory twinge of misgiving, but there was nothing to be done about it. Besides, it was, as Mary had said, getting late.

'Well, time you were off to bed now, Matthew,' I said. 'Thanks for telling us about the pictures. May we keep them down here a bit so that we can look at them again?'

'All right, but please don't lose them,' he agreed. His eye fell on the famine-victim portrait. 'That isn't a bit like you, Daddy. It really isn't,' he assured me. Then he said his good nights, and ran away upstairs.

We sat and looked at one another.

Mary's eyes slowly brimmed with tears.

'Oh, David. He was such a lovely little boy . . .'

Later, when she was calmer, she said:

'I'm afraid for him, David. This – this whatever it is, is getting more real to him. He's beginning to let it take control of him. . . . I'm afraid for him . . .'

I shook my head.

'I'm sure you've got it wrong. It isn't like that, you know. He was pretty emphatic that he is the one who decides when and whether it shall happen at all,' I pointed out.

'Naturally he'd *think* that,' she said.

I went on doing my best to soothe her anxiety. It didn't, I pointed out, make Matthew unhappy, not a bit. He'd had the sense not to tell any of his young friends about it, so there was no persecution element. Polly did not believe in Chocky at all, and preferred to regard the whole thing as a kind of forgery of Piff. He really was just an ordinary boy of his age – plus something he chose to call

Chocky, and we really did not have a scrap of evidence that this Chocky was doing him any harm at all . . .

I might just as well have saved my breath . . .

I looked in on him on my way to bed. He was asleep, with the light still on. A book he had been reading lay as it had dropped from his hands, face down on his chest. I read the title, then bent a little closer to make sure I had read aright. It was my copy of Lewis Mumford's *Living in Cities*. I picked it up, and in doing so woke Matthew.

'I don't wonder you fell asleep. A bit heavy for bedtime reading, isn't it?'

'Pretty boring,' he acknowledged. 'But Chocky thinks it's interesting – the parts of it I can understand for her.'

'Oh,' I said. 'Well . . . well, time to go to sleep now. Good night, old man.'

'Good night, Daddy.'

Seven

For our holiday that summer we took a cottage jointly
with Alan and Phyl Froome. They had married a couple
of years after we did, and had two children, Emma and
Paul, much of an age with our own. It was an arrangement, we thought, which would give the adults opportunities to go off duty for a bit, and have some holiday
themselves.

The place was Bontgoch, a village on an estuary in
North Wales, where I had enjoyed several holidays in my
own childhood. In those days it was simply a small grey
village with a few larger houses outside it. During summer
it had a scatter of visitors who were for the most part the
children and grandchildren of the owners of the larger
houses; they affected it very little. Since then it has been
discovered, and bungalows now dot the shoreline and the
lower slopes about the village. Their occupants are mostly
seasonal, transitory, or retired, and during the milder
months the majority are addicted to messing about with
boats. I had not expected that. Bontgoch is by no means
ideally situated for it, for the tides run fast in the estuary
and navigation can be tricky; but the crowded state of
the small boat world with its five-year queues for moorings
in many more favoured waters had overridden the dis-
advantages. Now it even had a painted-up shed with a
bar at one end called the Yacht Club.

We were, perhaps, a little odd in not having even one
boat amongst us, but for all that we enjoyed it. The sands
are still there for children to dabble around on at low
tide and catch shrimps and flat fish. So, too, on both sides
of the estuary are the not-too-steep mountains on which

one can climb and explore the pockings of old workings fascinatingly reputed to have been gold mines. It was good to be able to go off in the car for the day and leave Phyl and Alan in charge of the children – and quite good, too, to take charge when it was their turn for freedom. Everything was, in fact, a great success – until the Monday of the second week . . .

On that day it was Mary and I who were free. We drove almost off the map by very minor roads, left the car, walked along a hillside and picnicked by a stream with the whole Irish Sea spread out below us. In the evening we had a good dinner at a roadside hotel and dawdled back to Bontgoch about ten o'clock. We paused a moment by the gate to admire the serenity of a superb sunset, and then went up the path.

One had only to set foot on the threshold of the cottage to know that something had gone wrong. Mary sensed it at once. She stared at Phyl.

'What is it?' she said. 'What's happened?'

'It's all right, Mary. It's quite all right,' Phyl said. 'They're perfectly safe and sound. Both upstairs in bed now. Nothing to worry about.'

'What happened?' Mary said again.

'They fell in the river. But they're quite all right.'

She and Mary went upstairs. Alan reached for a bottle and poured a couple of whiskies.

'What's been going on?' I said as he held a glass towards me.

'It's quite all right now, as Phyl said,' he assured me. 'Near thing, though. Shook us to our foundations, I can tell you. Not stopped sweating yet.' He pressed a handkerchief to his brow as if in evidence, said 'Cheers', and downed half his glass.

I looked at him, and looked at the bottle. It had been untouched that morning, now it was three-quarters empty.

'But what happened?' I insisted.

He put down his glass, shook his head, and explained:

'Pure accident, old man. They were all four of them playing around on that rickety landing stage. The tide was a bit past the turn, and running out fast. That hulking motor-boat of Bill Weston's was moored about fifty yards up-stream. According to old Evans who saw the whole thing its mooring line must have broken. He says it came down too fast to be dragging. Anyway, it socked the landing-stage at full tilt, and the far end of the damned thing collapsed. My two happened to be standing back a bit, so they were only knocked down, but your two went straight into the water . . .'

He paused, exasperatingly. But for the repeated assurances that they were quite all right I could have shaken him. He took another swig at his glass.

'Well, you know the way it runs on the ebb. They were yards away in a few seconds. At first Evans thought they were done for, then he saw Matthew strike out towards Polly. He didn't see any more because he started haring off to the Yacht Club to give the alarm.

'It was Colonel Summers who went after them, but even with that fast motor-boat of his they were well over a mile downstream before he found them. Matthew was still supporting Polly.

'The old boy was tremendously impressed. He says that if he ever saw anything that deserved a medal, that did; and he's going to make sure Matthew gets one.

'We were in here when it happened. My two never thought to tell us until they had seen the Colonel's boat chase off after them. Not that we could have done anything. But lord-oh-lord, waiting for him to come back. . . . I hope I never have to spend an hour like that again . . .

'Anyway, it came out all right, thank God – and thanks to young Matthew. There's no doubt at all your Polly'd have been a goner, but for him. Damn good show, and if the Colonel needs any backing for that medal idea, he'll certainly get mine. Here's all the best to him: he deserves it.'

Alan finished off his drink at a gulp, and reached for the bottle again.

I finished mine, too. I felt I needed it.

Everybody ought to be able to swim. It had worried me at times for the last year or two that Matthew could never succeed in swimming more than three consecutive strokes . . .

I was shushed away from the room Polly was sharing with young Emma.

'She's fast asleep,' Mary told me. 'She's got a nasty bruise on her right shoulder. We think she must have hit the boat as she fell. Otherwise she seems only tired out. Oh, David . . .'

'It's all right, darling. It's over now.'

'Yes, thank God. Phyl told me all about it. But, David, how did Matthew do it . . . ?'

I looked in on Matthew. The light was still on. He was lying on his back staring at it. I had time to catch his worried look before he turned his head and saw me.

'Hullo, Daddy,' he said.

Momentarily he looked pleased, and relieved, but the anxious expression soon came back.

'Hullo, Matthew. How are you feeling?' I asked.

'All right,' he told me. 'We got jolly cold, but Auntie Phyl made us have a hot bath.'

I nodded. He certainly looked all right now.

'I've been hearing great things about you, Matthew,' I told him.

His look of worry grew more marked. His eyes dropped, and his fingers began twisting at the sheet. He looked up again.

'It's not true, Daddy,' he said, with great earnestness.

'It did rather make me wonder,' I admitted. 'A few days ago you couldn't swim.'

'I know, Daddy, but . . .' Again he twisted at the sheet. '. . . but Chocky can . . .' he finished, looking up at me uncertainly.

I tried to show nothing but sympathetic interest.

'Tell me about it,' I suggested.

Matthew looked a little relieved.

'Well, it all happened terribly quickly. I saw the boat just going to hit, and then I was in the water. I tried to swim, but I was awfully frightened because I knew it would be no good, and I thought I was going to be drowned. Then Chocky told me not to be a fool, and not to panic. She was sort of fierce. She sounded rather like Mr Caffer when he gets angry in class, only more. I've never known her get like that before, and I was so surprised that I stopped panicking. Then she said: "Now think of nothing, like you do with painting." So I tried. And then I was swimming. . . .' He frowned. 'I don't know how, but somehow she showed my arms and legs the way to swim, just like she makes my hands go the right way to draw. So, you see, it was really *her*, not me that did it, Daddy.'

'I see,' I said. It was a memorable overstatement. Matthew went on.

'You, and lots of other people, have shown me *how* to swim, Daddy, and I tried, but it kept on not happening until Chocky did it.'

'I see,' I lied again. I reflected for some moments while Matthew watched my face attentively.

'I see,' I said once more, and nodded. 'So, of course once you found you could swim, you struck out for the shore?'

Matthew's attentive look turned to an incredulous stare.

'But I couldn't do that. There was Polly. She'd fallen in, too.'

I nodded again.

'Yes,' I said. 'There was Polly, too – that does rather seem to me to be the point . . .'

Matthew considered. I think he went back to those first frightened moments in the water, for he shuddered slightly. Then his face took a look of determination.

'But it was Chocky who did it,' he asserted, obstinately.

Alan met my eye uneasily the next morning.

'I'm afraid I – well, it was the tension, I suppose. Waiting for that bloody boat to come back.... It seemed hours. ... Not knowing whether he'd found them.... Not able to do a damn thing about it. ... Bit of a reaction, I'm afraid ...'

'Forget it,' I told him. 'I'd have felt the same myself.'

We sat in the sun, waiting for the call to breakfast.

'What's getting me,' Alan said presently, 'is how did he do it? According to the Colonel he was still supporting her when the boat came up with them. Nearly a mile and a half, he reckons, in that fast ebb. Matthew was tired, he says, but not exhausted. And only a couple of days ago he was telling me, as if he were ashamed of it, too, that he couldn't swim.... I tried to teach him, but he didn't have the knack.'

'It's quite true. He couldn't,' I told him, and then, since he knew already about the Chocky problem and been responsible for bringing Landis into it, I gave him Matthew's version of the affair. He looked at me incredulously.

'But – well, hang it, and no disrespect to Matthew – but do you believe that?'

'I believe that Matthew believes it – and how else can one explain it? Besides ...' I told him about the pictures. He'd not heard of them before. 'They, somehow, make it not quite as difficult to accept, or half-accept,' I said.

Alan became thoughtful. He lit a cigarette, and sat silently smoking it, gazing out across the estuary. At last he said:

'If this is what it seems to be – and I can see that it's difficult to explain it any other way – it opens up a whole new phase of this Chocky business.'

'That's what we thought,' I acknowledged. 'And poor Mary's not at all happy about it. She's afraid for him.'

Alan shook his head.

'I can't see that she needs to be. After all, whether Chocky exists or not – and Landis, incidently seems to think that in some way she does – but whether she does, or not, it is because Matthew *believes* she does that your two are alive today. Does Mary realize that? It ought to help her a bit.'

'It ought,' I agreed. 'But – oh, I don't know – why do people always find it easier to believe in evil spirits than in good ones?'

'Self-preservation?' he suggested. 'It's safer to treat the unknown as inimical until it has proved itself. Hence the instinctive opposition to change. Perhaps this Chocky is in the process of proving itself. It doesn't seem to have made a bad start, either.'

I nodded. I said:

'I wish Mary could see it that way – but she worries . . .'

Matthew was late for lunch. I went in search of him, and found him sitting on the remains of the wrecked jetty, talking to a good-looking, fair-haired young man I did not remember seeing before. Matthew looked up as I approached.

'Hullo, Daddy – oh, is it late?'

'It is,' I told him.

The young man got up, politely.

'I'm sorry, sir. I'm afraid it's my fault for keeping him, I should have thought. I was just asking him about his exploit: he's quite a local hero, you know, after yesterday.'

'Maybe,' I said, 'but he still has to eat. Come along now, Matthew.'

'Good-bye,' Matthew said to the young man, and we turned back to the cottage.

'Who was that?' I asked.

'Just a man,' said Matthew. 'He wanted to know how Polly is after yesterday. He said he's got a little girl just like her, so he was interested.'

It did just cross my mind that the stranger looked a little young to be a family man of ten or eleven years' standing, but then you never know nowadays, and by the time lunch was finished I had forgotten about the incident.

During the next few days Matthew developed such a passion for swimming that he could scarcely be kept away from the water.

Then the holiday was over. Colonel Summers dropped in on the last evening for a drink, and to assure me that he had already written to The Royal Swimming Society commending Matthew.

'Plucky youngster of yours. Good reason to be proud of him. Could just as easily have looked after number one: many would. Funny thing his pretending he couldn't swim; unaccountable things, boys. Never mind. Damned good show! And good luck to him.'

The following Monday evening I got home late and tired after a busy day catching up with the accumulation of work at the office. I was vaguely aware that Mary was a little distrait, but she had the tact to keep the cause to herself until I had eaten my supper. Then she produced a newspaper, much folded for post, and handed it to me.

'Came this afternoon,' she said. 'Front page.' Her expression as she watched me unfold it and read MERIO-NETH MERCURY across the top was disquieting.

'Further down,' she said.

I looked at the lower half of the page and saw a photograph of Matthew looking back at me. Not at all a bad photograph either. I looked at the headline to the story beside it. It said:

BOY-HERO TELLS OF 'GUARDIAN ANGEL' RESCUE. My heart sank a little. I read on:

'Matthew Gore (12) of Hindmere, Surrey, on holiday at Bontgoch has been nominated to receive a medal for his bravery in saving his sister Polly (10) from drowning in the estuary of the Afon Cyfrwys at Bontgoch last Monday.

'Matthew and his sister were playing on a light wooden jetty not far from the Bontgoch Yacht Club when a motor-cruiser belonging to Mr William Weston, a local resident, was torn from its moorings by the force of the ebb tide, and crashed into the jetty, demolishing ten feet of it, and hurling both children into the swirling current.

'Matthew immediately struck out, and, seizing his sister, supported her head above water as the flood bore them away. The alarm was given by Mr Evan Evans, a familiar figure in Bontgoch, whereupon Colonel Summers, a well-known local resident, hastened to the scene and lost no time in giving chase in his motor-cruiser.

'Colonel Summers was compelled to pursue the two children nearly two miles down the treacherous waters of the estuary before he was able to manoeuvre his boat alongside them so that they could be safely grappled aboard.

'Said the Colonel: "Matthew undoubtedly saved his sister's life at the risk of his own. England could do with more boys like him."

'Most astounding fact of all: *Matthew did not know he could swim.*

'Interviewed by our reporter he modestly denied any claims to heroism. "Polly could not swim, and when I found I could, the obvious thing was to help her," he said. Questioned about this, he told our reporter that he had taken swimming lessons, but had never been able to learn to swim. "When I was suddenly thrown into the water I was terrified," he acknowledged, "but then I heard a voice telling me to keep calm, and how to move my arms and legs. So I did as it said, and found I could swim."

'There seems to be no doubt that Matthew is telling the truth. Our reporter was unable to find anyone who had seen him swimming before that, and it was generally thought that he could not swim.

'Asked if he was not astonished to hear a voice speaking to him, he replied that he had often heard it before, and so did not find it very surprising.

'When our reporter suggested that it could be the voice of his Guardian Angel, he admitted that it might be that.

'However unlikely the prospect of "instant swimming" taught by a spiritual instructor may seem, there can be no doubt that Matthew performed an heroic action by the bravery he showed in saving his sister's life at the risk of his own, and it is to be hoped he will be awarded the medal he so richly deserves.'

I looked up at Mary. She shook her head slowly. I shrugged.

'Shall we . . . ?' I began to suggest.

Mary shook her head again.

'He'll be fast asleep by now. Besides, what's the point? It's done now.'

'It's only a local paper,' I said. 'But how on earth . . . ?' Then I remembered the young man who had been talking to Matthew on the shore . . .

'They've got Hindmere,' Mary pointed out. 'They've only got to look in the telephone directory.'

I was determined to be hopeful.

'Why should they bother? It reads like a pretty phoney sensation worked up by a local reporter, anyway.'

I don't think either of us was quite certain just then whom we meant by this off-stage 'they', but it did not take long for me to discover that I was underestimating the enterprise of modern communications.

I have fallen into the bad habit of switching on the radio as a background to shaving – bad because untroubled shaving is itself a good background for thinking – however, that's modern life, and the next morning I turned on 'Today' as usual, and listened patiently while a professor from the latest Midland university explained how his excavations proved that the Kingdom of Mercia had at one time encompassed the town of Montgomery. Then, when he had finished, Jack de Manio said: 'The time is *exactly* twenty-five and a half minutes past eight – no, hang it, I mean past seven. Well now, from the influence of ancient Angles to the incidence of a modern Angel. Young Matthew Gore while on holiday from his home at Hindmere, recently, and gallantly, saved his still younger sister from drowning, and the peculiar thing is that young Matthew had never swum before. Dennis Clutterbuck reports:'

The quality of the transmission changed. A voice said:

'I am told that when an accident flung you and your sister into the fast-flowing river Cyfrwys at Bontgoch you immediately went to her rescue and supported her in the water until you were picked up more than a mile downstream. Is that so?'

'Well, yes,' said Matthew's voice. He sounded a little doubtful.

'And they also tell me you had never swum before?'

'Yes – I mean, no,' said Matthew, in some confusion.

'You hadn't ever swum before?'

'No,' said Matthew, definitely now. 'I'd tried, but it wouldn't happen . . .' he added.

'But this time it did?'

'Yes,' said Matthew.

'I am told you heard a voice telling you what to do?'

Matthew hesitated. 'Well – sort of . . .' he conceded.

'And you think this must have been the voice of your Guardian Angel?'

'No,' said Matthew indignantly. 'That's a lot of rot.'

'But you told the local reporter . . .'

Matthew interrupted him.

'I didn't. *He* said it, and I didn't know he was a reporter, anyway.'

'But you did hear a voice?'

Matthew hesitated again. Once more he could manage no better than:

'. . . Sort of.'

'And after you had heard it, you found you were able to swim?'

A grunt from Matthew.

'But now you don't think it was your Guardian Angel that told you how to do it?'

'I never said anything about Guardian Angels – it was *him*.' Matthew sounded exasperated. 'All that happened was that I got into a flap, and Chock. . . .' He stopped abruptly. I could almost hear him bite his tongue. 'I just found I could swim,' he ended lamely.

The interviewer started to speak again but was cut off in the middle of the first syllable.

Jack de Manio said:

'Swimming in one easy lesson. Well, whether there was a Guardian Angel involved, or not, congratulations to Matthew on the way he put the lesson to use.'

Matthew came down to his breakfast as I was finishing mine.

'I've just been listening to you on the wireless,' I told him.

'Oh,' said Matthew. He did not seem disposed to follow that up, and attended to his cornflakes, rather apprehensively.

'When did it happen?' I inquired.

'A man rang up, when Mummy was out. He said was I Matthew, and I said I was, and he said he was BBC, and could he come round and see me. I said I supposed it'd be all right, because it seemed rude to say no to the BBC. So he came; and he showed me a bit about me in the paper. Then he turned on his recorder, and asked me questions. And after that he went away again.'

'And you didn't tell Mummy, or anyone else, that he'd been?'

He dabbled his cornflakes.

'Well, you see, I thought she'd be afraid that I'd told him about Chocky – though I didn't. And I didn't think it would be interesting enough to get broadcasted, anyway.'

Not very valid reasons, I thought. Probably he was feeling guilty over letting the man into the house at all.

'H'm. – It can't be helped now,' I said. 'But if there are any more would-be interviewers, I think you'd better refer them to Mummy, or me, before you talk to them. Will you do that?'

'Okay, Daddy,' he agreed, and then added, with a

frown. 'It's a bit difficult though. You see, I didn't know the man at Bontgoch was a reporter; and the BBC one – well, it didn't seem like an *interview* exactly.'

'Perhaps the simplest way would be to treat any stranger as a suspected interviewer,' I suggested. 'You might easily make a slip, and we don't want them getting on to Chocky, do we?'

Matthew's mouth was now too full of cornflakes to let him speak, but his nod concurred very decisively.

Eight

A young man representing, as he put it, the *Hindmere and District Courier* turned up that afternoon. Mary dealt with him briskly. Yes, she had seen that rubbish about a guardian angel, and was surprised that a paper had printed such nonsense. Matthew had had swimming lessons, but had lacked the confidence to trust himself to the water. What had happened was that in the emergency he had known what he *ought* to do to swim; he had made the motions he had been taught to make, and discovered that he *could* swim. He had been very brave in going to the rescue of his sister, and very fortunate, but there was nothing miraculous about it. No, she was sorry he couldn't see Matthew; he was out for the day. And, in any case, she preferred not to have him troubled about it. After considerable persuasion the reporter went away, ill-satisfied.

The same day Landis rang me up at the office. He had, he said been thinking about Matthew, and a number of questions had occurred to him. My first thought was that he was about to offer to come down again, which would not please Mary; fortunately, however, that was not his idea, at the moment, at any rate; instead, he suggested that I should have dinner with him one evening. It crossed my mind to ask him if he had heard Matthew on 'Today' that morning, but I had no wish to get involved in a lot of explanation in the middle of a busy day, so I did not mention it. In the circumstances I could scarcely refuse his invitation, and it also occurred to me that he might have thought of a suitable consultant. We agreed to meet at his Club the following Thursday.

I got back to find Mary preparing our dinner with grim

resolve and a heavy hand, as she does when she is put out. I inquired why.

'Matthew's been talking to reporters again,' she said, punishing the saucepan.

'But I told him . . .'

'I know,' she said bitterly. 'Oh, it isn't his fault, poor boy, but it does make me so wild.'

I inquired further.

Reporters, it seemed, was a manner of speaking. There had been only one reporter. Matthew, on his way home, had encountered him at the end of the road. He had asked if he was speaking to Matthew Gore, and introduced himself as the representative of the *Hindmere and District Courier*. Matthew told him he must speak to his mother first. Oh, of course, agreed the young man, that was only proper, naturally he had called on Mrs Gore to ask her permission. He had been hoping to have a talk with Matthew there at the house, only he had not been at home. But it was very fortunate that they had met like this. They couldn't really talk, standing here on the corner, though. What about some tea and cakes in the café over there? So they had adjourned to the café.

'You must write to the editor at once. It's disgusting,' she told me.

I wrote a suitably indignant letter, without the least hope that it would be heeded, but it helped to reduce Mary's feelings to a mere simmer. Rather than risk raising the temperature again I refrained from mentioning Landis's call.

Wednesday passed without incident – well, when I say 'without incident', there was a letter in the morning post addressed to Matthew and bearing a printed inscription in the left-hand corner: 'The Psychenomenon Circle', which I thought it judicious to abstract, and pocket.

I read it in the train later. The writer had heard on the radio a very brief reference to Matthew's unusual experience, and felt convinced that a more detailed account was likely to be of great interest to the members of his circle who were interested in psychic experiences and phenomena of all kinds. If Matthew would care to – etc., etc . . .

But, if Wednesday was undisturbing, Thursday made up for it.

I was in the act of transferring my attention from *The Times* personal column to the leader page, an almost anti-social exercise in a full railway compartment, when my eye was caught by a photograph in the copy of the *Daily Telegraph* held by the man in the opposite seat. Even at a glance it had a quality which triggered my curiosity. I leant forward to take a closer look. Habitual travellers develop an instinct which warns them of such liberties. My vis-à-vis immediately lowered his paper to glare at me as if I were committing trespass and probably worse, and ostentatiously refolded it to present a different page.

The glimpse I had had, brief though it was, disturbed me enough to send me to the Waterloo Station bookstall in search of a *Telegraph* I could rightfully read. They had, of course, sold out. This somehow helped to convince me that my suspicions were well founded, and on arriving in Bloomsbury Square I lost no time in sending a message round the office requesting the loan of a copy of today's *Telegraph*. Eventually one was unearthed, and brought to me. I unfolded it with a sense of misgiving – and I was right to feel it . . .

Half a page was devoted to photographs of pictures on display at an exhibition entitled 'Art and the Schoolchild'. The one that had caught my eye on the train caught it again, and reduced the rest to scribbles. It was a scene from an upper window showing half a dozen boys laden with satchels jostling their way towards an open gate in a wall. The boys had an angular, spindly look; curious to some no doubt, but familiar to me. I had no need to read the print beneath the photograph, but I did:

'"Homeward" by Matthew Gore (12) of Hinton School, Hindmere, reveals a talent and power of observation quite outstanding in one of his age.'

I was still looking at it when Tommy Percell, one of my partners came in, and glanced over my shoulder.

'Ah, yes,' he told me. 'Spotted that on the way up this morning. Congratulations. Thought it must be your youngster. Didn't know he'd a gift for that kind of thing. Very clever – but a bit queer, though, isn't it?'

'Yes,' I said, with a feeling that the thing was slipping out of my hands. 'Yes, it is a bit queer . . .'

Landis drank half his sherry at a gulp.

'Seen the papers?' he inquired.

I did not pretend to misunderstand him.

'Yes, I saw today's *Telegraph*,' I admitted.

'But not the *Standard*? They've got it, too – with a paragraph about a child-artist of genius. You didn't tell me about this,' he added, with reproach.

'I didn't know about it when I last saw you.'

'Nor about the swimming?'

'It hadn't happened then.'

'Both Chocky, of course?'

'Apparently,' I said.

He ruminated a moment.

'A bit rash, wasn't it? Putting this picture in for exhibition, I mean.'

'Not rash – Unauthorized,' I told him.

'Pity,' he said, and ordered a couple more sherries.

'That picture,' he went on. 'The figures have a curious, attenuated, not to say scrawny look. Is that characteristic?'

I nodded.

'How are they done?'

I told him what Matthew had told Mary and me. It did not appear to surprise him, but he fell into rumination again. He emerged from it to say:

'It's not only the figures. All the verticals are exaggerated. It's almost as if they were seen by someone accustomed to different proportions – to a broader, squatter view so that it seems. . . .' He broke off, staring expressionlessly at his glass for a moment. Then his face took on a look of sudden illumination. 'No, it isn't, by God. It's like looking through slightly distorting glasses, and painting what you see, without compensation. I bet you that if you were to look at that picture through a pair of glasses which diminished the verticals only it would appear to have normal proportion. – It's as if Chocky's perception can't compensate adequately for the characteristics of Matthew's eyes . . .'

'I don't follow that,' I said, after a moment's thought. 'The eyes that are seeing the view are also seeing the picture. Surely the two distortions ought to cancel out?'

'It was an analogy – or nearly – and maybe I was oversimplifying,' he conceded, 'but I'll be surprised if it isn't something along those lines. Let's go and have dinner, shall we?'

Over the meal he inquired in detail into the swimming incident. I told him as much as I could, and he clearly found it no less significant than the painting. What astonished me most of the time, and still more on later reflection, was his lack of surprise. It was so marked that I almost had a suspicion for a time that he might be humouring me – leading me on to see how far I would go in my claims for Matthew, but I had to abandon that. I could detect no trace of scepticism; he appeared to accept the fantastic without prejudice.

Gradually I began to get a feeling that he was away ahead of me; that while I was still in the stage of reluctantly conceding Chocky's existence as an unavoidable hypothesis, he had passed me, and was treating it as an established fact. It was rather, I thought, as if he had applied Sherlock Holmes' dictum: 'When you have eliminated the impossible, whatever remains, *however improbable*, must be the truth'; and had thorough confidence in the finding that the formula had produced. For some reason that I couldn't quite determine, it had the effect of slightly increasing my disquiet.

After dinner, over coffee and brandy, Landis said:

'As I expect you'll have gathered, I've been giving the

problem considerable thought, and in my opinion Thorbe is your man. Sir William Thorbe. He's a very sound fellow with great experience – and not bigoted, which is something in our profession. I mean, he's not an out and out psycho-analyst, for instance. He treats his cases on their merits – if he decides analysis will help, then he'll use it; if he thinks it calls for one of the new drugs, then he'll use that. He has a large number of quite remarkable successes to his credit. I don't think you could do better than to get his opinion, if he's willing to take Matthew on. I'm certain that if anyone can help it's Thorbe.'

I did not greatly care for that 'if anyone', but let it pass. I said:

'I seem to remember that the last time we met you were doubtful whether Matthew needed help.'

'My dear fellow, I still am. But your wife does, you know. And you yourself could do with some definite assurance, couldn't you?'

And, of course, he was right. Mary and I were a lot more worried about Matthew than Matthew was about himself. Just the knowledge that we were doing our best for him by taking competent advice would relieve our minds.

In the end I agreed that, subject to Mary's consent, I would be glad to have Sir William Thorbe's opinion.

'Good,' said Landis. 'I'll have a word with him. I'm pretty sure that in the circumstances he'll be keen to see Matthew. If he will, I'm sure you'll get as good a diagnosis as anyone can give you. I'll be able to let you know – in a few days, I hope.'

And on that, we parted.

I arrived home to find Mary erupting with indignation. I gathered she had seen the *Evening Standard*.

'It's outrageous!' she announced, as if my arrival had pressed a siphon lever. 'What right had she to send the thing in without even consulting us? The least she could have done was to *ask* us. To enter it like that without your even knowing! – It's sort of – what do they call it?

– invasion of privacy. . . . She didn't even ask Matthew. Just sent it off without telling anybody. I shouldn't have thought she'd have dared do such a thing without getting *somebody's* consent. I don't know what some of these teachers are coming to. They seem to think they have all the rights over the children's lives, and the parents have none. Really, the kind of people these Teachers' Training Colleges turn out these days. . . . You'd have thought that out of ordinary courtesy and consideration for a child's parents' point of view. . . . No manners at all. . . . How can you expect a child to learn decent behaviour when he's taught by people who don't know how to behave . . .? It's quite disgraceful. I want you to write a really stiff letter to the headmaster tomorrow telling him just what we think of her behaviour, and demanding an apology. . . . No, do it now, tonight. You won't have time in the morning . . .'

I'd had a tiring day.

'She wouldn't apologize. Why on earth should she?' I said.

Mary stared at me, took a breath and started off again. I cut it short.

'She was doing her job. One of her pupils produced a picture that she thought good enough to submit for this exhibition. She wanted him to have the credit for it. Naturally, she thought we'd be delighted, and so we should have been – but for this Chocky business.'

'She ought to have asked our consent . . .'

'So that you could explain to her about Chocky, and tell her why we didn't want it shown? And, anyway, it was right at the end of the term. She probably had just time to send it in before she went away. I wouldn't mind betting at this very moment she's expecting to receive a letter of thanks and congratulation from us.'

Mary made an angry sound regrettably like a snort.

'All right,' I told her. 'You go ahead and write the head-master that letter. You won't get your apology. What are you going to do then, make a row? Local newspapers love rows between parents and schoolteachers. So do the national ones. If you want more publicity for the picture than they've already printed you'll certainly get it. And somebody's going to point out that the Matthew Gore who painted the picture is the same one who is the guardian angel hero. – Someone's going to do that anyway, but do we want it done on a national scale? How long will it take before Chocky is right out of the bag?'

Mary's look of dismay made me sorry for the way I'd put it. She went on staring at me for several seconds, then her face suddenly crumpled. I picked her up and carried her over to the armchair . . .

After a time she pulled the handkerchief out of my breast-pocket. Gradually I felt her relax. One hand sought, and found, mine.

'I'm sorry to be so silly,' she said.

I hugged her.

'It's all right, darling. You're not silly, you're anxious – and I don't wonder.'

'But I *was* silly. I didn't see what making a row might lead to.' She paused, kneading the handkerchief in her clenched right hand. 'I'm so afraid for Matthew,' she said unsteadily. She raised herself a little, and looked into my face. 'David, tell me something honestly. . . . They – they won't think he – he's mad, will they, David . . . ?'

'Of course not, darling. How could they possibly? You couldn't find a saner boy anywhere than Matthew, you know that.'

'But if they find out about Chocky? If they get to know that he thinks he hears her speaking . . . ? I mean, hearing voices in your head . . . that's. . . .' She let it tail away.

'Darling,' I told her. 'You're being afraid of the wrong thing. Put that right away. There is nothing – nothing at all – wrong with Matthew himself. He's as sane and sensible a boy as one could wish to meet. Please, please get it into your head quite firmly that this Chocky, whatever it is, is not subjective – it is objective. It does not come *from* Matthew, it is something outside that comes

98

to him. I know it's hard to believe, because one doesn't understand how it can happen. But I'm quite convinced it is so, and so is Landis. He's an expert on mental disorders, and he's thoroughly satisfied that Matthew is not suffering from any aberration. You must believe that.'

'I do try, but ... I don't understand. What *is* Chocky ...? The swimming ... the painting ... all the questions ...?'

'That's what we don't know – yet. My own idea is that Matthew is – well, sort of haunted. I know that's an unfortunate word, it carries ideas of fear and malevolence, but I don't mean that at all. It's just that there isn't another word for it. What I am thinking of is a kindly sort of haunting. ... It quite clearly doesn't mean Matthew any harm. It's only alarming to us because we don't understand it. Doing my best to think of it objectively it seems to me we're being a bit ungrateful. After all, remember, Matthew thinks it saved both their lives. ... And if it didn't, we don't know what did.

'Whatever it is, I think we'd be wrong to regard it as a threat. It seems intrusive and inquisitive, but basically well disposed – essentially a benign kind of – er – presence.'

'Oh, I see,' said Mary. 'In fact you're trying to tell me it *is* a guardian angel?'

'No – er – well, I suppose I mean – er – yes, in a way ... I said.

Nine

I bought a copy of the *Hindmere & District Courier* at the
station bookstall the next morning. As I expected, it was
there; in the fourth column on the front page under the
heading 'GUARDIAN ANGEL' SAVES CHILDREN.
The quotes around 'guardian angel' to show that the
editor wasn't committing himself caused me an initial
misgiving, but it subsided considerably as I read on. Local
papers, wisely perhaps, are not in the habit of taking the
mickey out of local residents, other than certain well-
established figures of fun who enjoy it. I had to admit that
the piece was skilfully done, objective in tone, though with
unmistakable reservations on the writer's part, and yet
with a trace of genuine puzzlement showing through here
and there; rather as if he had decided to treat this evidence
of the crackpot fringe with kindness, and had then become
uncertain what the evidence was showing. The guardian
angel angle was left almost entirely to the headline; the
whole account gave the impression that something quite
unusual had certainly happened when Matthew found
himself in the water, but nobody knew quite what. There
was no doubt, however, that Matthew had bravely
rescued Polly.

And in all, since the young man had had to do his job,
it was fair enough, and a lot better than I had feared.
Apart from the headline, indeed, there was little to com-
plain of. But unfortunately people notice headlines; after
all, that's what they're there for.

Alan rang up in the morning and suggested lunch, so I
joined him.

'Saw the photograph of Matthew's picture in the paper

yesterday,' he said. 'After what you'd told us about the pictures I thought I'd look in at the exhibition. It's only a few doors from our office. Most of it's the usual crummy stuff. I don't wonder they picked out Matthew's. Rummy sort of vision though, all kind of elongated – and yet it's got something, you know.' He paused, and looked at me curiously. 'After all you and Mary have said about Chocky I wonder you sent it in.'

'We didn't,' I told him, and explained.

'Oh, I see. Bit unfortunate, coming on top of the other,' he said. 'By the way, I had a visit from one of the Swimming Society people on Wednesday. Just checking up on Colonel Summers' recommendation for a medal, he said. Apparently the Society had heard from somewhere that Matthew had never swum before. That seemed to them to cast a doubt on the whole story – and no wonder, either. So I told him what I knew about it. Then he wanted to know if it was true about the non-swimming. I had to say yes. Damn it, I was trying to teach him to swim only a couple of days before. I think he believed me, but the poor fellow went away more puzzled than ever.' He paused again, and went on:

'You know, with all this, David, Chocky's right in the wings. She'll be taking her call any moment now. What are you going to do about it?'

I shrugged. 'About *it* what can I do except try to deal with things as they crop up? About Matthew, though, Landis has come up with a recommendation.' I told him what Landis had said.

'Thorbe – Thorbe, with a handle,' Alan muttered, frowning. 'I heard something about him just the other day – Oh, yes. I know. He's recently got an appointment as a sort of advisory industrial psychologist to one of the big groups. Can't remember which, but one of the really big boys. Fellow who told me was wondering what whacking retainer he gets for that – on top of a thumping good practice.'

'Oh,' I said. 'At thumping good fees?'

Alan shook his head.

'Can't tell you about that, but he won't be cheap. I should have a word with Landis about it before you commit yourself.'

'Thanks, I will. One hears such things. I don't want to be landed with a thumping good fee that goes on for months and months, if it can be helped.'

'I shouldn't think you're likely to be let in for that. After all, nobody has suggested that there's anything *wrong* with Matthew, nothing that needs treatment. All you really want is an explanation to set your minds at rest – and advice on the best way to cope with things, isn't it?'

'I don't know,' I told him. 'I admit that this Chocky hasn't done him any harm . . .'

'And has, in fact, saved his and Polly's lives, don't forget.'

'Yes. But it's Mary I'm worried about now. She's not going to be easy in her mind until she's satisfied that Chocky has been driven right away, abolished, exorcized, or somehow finished with . . .'

Alan considered, and nodded.

'Security. . . . In mediocritate solus. . . . Normality above rubies. . . . Instinct overriding mind. . . . Well, we're not all made alike – men and women particularly. . . . But get her to wait for Thorbe's verdict, old man. I've a feeling it might lead to trouble if she tries to smoke out this Chocky off her own bat – if you'll excuse the expression.'

'She won't do that,' I told him. 'She knows it would antagonize Matthew. She's a bit like Polly in a way, both of them feel they've been alienated. She's afraid of making it worse, and afraid for Matthew, too. The devil of it is there doesn't seem to be anything one can do to help her.'

Alan shook his head.

'Not until you know more, old boy. And for that I think you'll have to pin your faith on Thorbe.'

I arrived home to find the atmosphere a trifle gloomy, perhaps, but certainly not critical. My spirits lifted. Mary must have read the *Courier*, and I judged, reacted to it much as I had. I asked about the day.

'I thought I'd keep clear of the town,' she told me, 'so I did the ordering by phone. About eleven o'clock a nice but dotty old clergyman called. He was disappointed to hear that Matthew was out because he had wanted to explain an error to him, but he decided to explain it to me instead. He was sorry to read, he said, that Matthew has been misled into attributing his survival to the intervention of a guardian angel, because the idea of a guardian angel was not a truly Christian conception. It was one of those pagan beliefs which the early church had neglected to suppress so that it, along with a number of other erroneous beliefs, had mistakenly and temporarily become incorporated in the true faith. A great many of the errors had been expelled by the true doctrine. This one, however, had been remarkably hardy, and it was the duty of all Christians to see to it that it was not perpetuated. So would I please do my part to fortify the faith by telling Matthew that his Maker did not depute these matters to amanuenses. It was He, and He alone, who could confer upon Matthew the ability to save himself, and the gift of courage to save his little sister. He considered it his duty to clear up this misunderstanding.

'So, of course, I told him I would, and just after he had gone Janet rang up.'

'Oh, no . . . !'

'Yes. She was thrilled about Matthew's success with the picture . . .'

'And wants to come over tomorrow to discuss it?'

'Well, actually, she said Sunday. It's Patience who rang up in the afternoon and said could she come tomorrow.'

'I hope,' I told her, without much hope, 'that you put them both off, firmly.'

She hesitated. 'Well, Janet's always so difficult and insistent . . .'

'Oh,' I said, and picked up the telephone.

'No, wait a minute,' she protested.

'I'm damned if we're going to sit here all the week-end listening to your sisters taking Matthew to pieces in a gloating orgy of dissection. You know just the line they'll take – gushing, inquisitive, self-congratulatory, phoney commiseration for their unfortunate sister who would have the ill-luck to have a peculiar child if any one did. To hell with it!' I put my finger on the dial.

'No,' said Mary. 'I'd better do it.'

I surrendered the handset.

'All right,' I agreed. 'Tell them they can't come. That I've fixed up for us to go out with friends tomorrow and Sunday – And next week-end, too, or they'll switch it to that if you give them the chance.'

She did, quite efficiently, and looked at me, as she put the phone down, with an air of relief that cheered me immensely.

'Thank you, David ...' she began. Then the phone rang. I picked it up and listened.

'No,' I said. 'He's in bed and asleep now.... No, he'll be out all day tomorrow,' and put it down again.

'What was that?' Mary asked.

'The *Sunday Dawn*, wanting an interview with Matthew.' I thought it over a moment. 'At a guess I'd say they've just tied up Matthew the life-saver with Matthew the artist. There'll probably be more of them.'

There were. The *Sunday Voice* followed by the *Report*.

'That settles it,' I told Mary. 'We'll *have* to go out tomorrow. And we'll have to start early, before they come camping in the front garden. I tell you what, we'll stay away over night. Let's go and pack.'

We started upstairs, and the phone went again. I hesitated.

'Oh, leave the thing,' said Mary.

So we did – and the next time.

We managed to get away by seven o'clock, unimpeded by interviewers, and set course for the coast.

'I hope they won't break in while we're away,' said Mary, 'I feel like a refugee.'

We all began to feel like refugees a couple of hours later as we neared the sea. The roads grew thick with cars, our speed was little better than a crawl. Mysterious hold-ups occurred, immobilizing everything for miles. The children began to get bored.

'It's all Matthew's fault,' Polly complained.

'It isn't,' Matthew denied. 'I didn't want any of it to happen. It just happened.'

'Then it's all Chocky's fault.'

'You ought to be jolly grateful to Chocky,' Matthew pointed out.

'I know, but I'm not. She spoils everything,' said Polly.

'The last time we came this way we had Piff with us. She was a bit of a nuisance,' I observed.

'Piff was just a silly. She didn't tell me things, I had to tell her. I bet Chocky's telling Matthew things now, or asking him her stupid questions.'

'As a matter of fact she's not. She's not been here since Tuesday. I think she's gone home,' Matthew retorted.

'Where's her home?' asked Polly.

'I don't know, but she was a bit worried. So I think she's gone home to ask about things.'

'What sort of things?' Polly wanted to know.

I grew conscious of Mary beside me taking no part.

'Well, if she's not here let's forget all about her for a bit,' I suggested.

Polly put her head out of the window and looked up and down the stationary line of cars.

'We aren't ever going to move. I shall read my book,' she announced. She dug it out from beside her, and opened it. Matthew looked down at the illustration.

'What's that supposed to be – a circus?' he inquired.

'Pooh,' Polly exclaimed in contempt. 'It's a very interesting story about a pony called Twinklehooves. He was in a circus three books ago, now he wants to be a ballet dancer.'

'Oh,' said Matthew with quite commendable restraint.

We arrived at a vast car park charging five shillings a time, collected our things and went in search of the sea. The pebbly beach near the park was crowded with groups clustering around contending transistor sets. So we made our way further along and down the pebbles, until all that separated us from the shining summer sea was a band of oil and ordure about six feet wide, and a fringe of scum along the water's edge.

'Oh, God,' said Mary. 'You're not going to bathe in *that*,' she told Matthew who was beginning to unbutton his shirt.

Matthew looked at the mess more closely; even he seemed a little dismayed.

'But I do want to swim now I can,' he protested.

'Not here,' said Mary. 'Oh, dear. It was a lovely beach only a few years ago. Now it's . . .'

'Just the edge of the Cloaca Britannica?' I suggested.

'Let's go somewhere else. Come along, we're moving,' I called to Matthew who was still staring down at the mess in a fascinated, dreamy way. I waited for him while Polly and Mary began to pick their way up the beach.

'Chocky's back, is she?' I asked as he came up.

'How did you know?' he inquired, with surprise.

'I recognized the signs. Look, do me a favour will you? Just keep her under cover if you can. We don't want to spoil Mummy's day – at least,' I added, 'not more than this place has already.'

'Okay,' he agreed.

We went a little inland and found a village nestled in a cleft at the foot of the Downs. It was peaceful. And there was an inn which gave us quite a passable lunch. I asked if we could stay the night, and found that by good luck they had rooms to spare. Mary and I lazed on deck-chairs in the garden. Matthew disappeared, saying vaguely that he was going to look round. Polly lay on the lawn under a tree, and identified herself with the ambitions of Twinkle-hooves. After an hour or so I suggested a stroll before tea.

We found a path which followed the contour across the side of the hill and walked it in a leisurely fashion. After about half a mile we rounded a shoulder and came in sight of a figure working intently on a large sketch-pad supported by his knees. I stopped. Mary said:

'It's Matthew.'

'Yes,' I agreed, and turned to go back.

'No,' she said. 'Let's go on. I'd like to see.'

Rather reluctantly I went forward with her. Matthew seemed quite unaware of us. Even when we drew close he remained utterly absorbed in his work. From a box of crayons on the grass beside him he would select what he wanted, with decision, and apply it to the paper with a deftness I could not recognize in him. Then, with a curious mixture of delicacy and firmness he smudged, blurred, and softened the line using his fingers, or his thumb, or a part of a grubby handkerchief on which he wiped his hands before adding the next stroke and rubbing that skilfully into the right tone and density.

The painting of a picture seems to me at any time a marvel, but to watch the Sussex landscape taking form on the paper from such crude materials under such an unfamiliar technique held me completely fascinated, and Mary, too. We must have stood there almost unmoving for more than half an hour before Matthew seemed to slump slightly as he relaxed. Then he lifted his head, sighed heavily, and lifted the finished picture to study it. Presently he became aware of us standing behind him, and turned his head.

'Oh, hullo,' he said, looking at Mary a little uncertainly.

'Oh, Matthew, that's beautiful,' she exclaimed.

Matthew looked relieved. He studied the picture again.

'I think Chocky's seeing things more properly now, though it's still a bit funny,' he said judicially.

Mary asked tentatively:

'Will you give it to me, Matthew? I promise to keep it very safely, if you will.'

Matthew looked up at her with a smile. He recognized a peace overture.

'Yes, if you like Mummy,' he said, and then added on a cautionary note. 'Only you'll have to be careful. This kind smudges if you don't spray them with something or other.'

'I'll be most careful. It's much too beautiful to spoil,' she assured him.

'Yes, it is rather beautiful,' Matthew agreed. 'Chocky thinks that, except where we've spoilt it, this is a very beautiful planet.'

We arrived home on Sunday evening feeling much the better for our week-end. Mary, however, was not looking forward to Monday.

'These newspaper men are so pushing. Foot in the door and all that,' she complained.

'I doubt if they'll trouble you much – not the Sundays, anyway. It'll have gone stale by next week-end. I think the best thing would be to get Matthew out of the way. It's only one day; he starts school again on Tuesday. Make him up some sandwiches and send him off with instructions to keep clear until six o'clock. See that he has enough money to go to the pictures if he gets bored. He'll be all right.'

'It seems a bit hard on him to be turned out.'

'I know, but I think he'd prefer that to interviewers badgering him about guardian angels.'

So next morning Mary shooed him out of the place – and just as well. Six callers inquired for Matthew in the course of the day. They were, our own vicar, another vaguely concerned clergyman, a middle-aged lady who confided with some intensity that she was a spiritualist, a member of the regional Arts-Group which she was sure Matthew would want to join, another lady who considered the dream-life of children to be a disgracefully neglected field of study, and an instructor at the local baths who hoped that Matthew would give a demonstration of life-saving at the next swimming gala.

I arrived home to find Mary quite exhausted.

'If ever I questioned the power of the press, I retract. I now just think it a pity that most of it seems to be exerted in the lunatic fringe,' she told me.

Apart from that, however, Monday was uneventful. Matthew appeared to have enjoyed his day out. He came back with two pictures, both landscapes from the same viewpoint. One was unmistakably Chocky-directed, the other less good, but Matthew was proud of it.

'I did it all myself,' he told us. 'Chocky's been telling me how to *look* at things, and I'm sort of beginning to see what she means.'

On Tuesday morning Matthew went off to school to start his new term. On Tuesday afternoon he returned home, with a black eye.

Mary regarded it with dismay.

'Oh, Matthew. You've been fighting,' she exclaimed.

'I haven't,' Matthew told her, indignantly. 'I was fought at.'

According to his account he had been simply standing in the playground during break when a slightly older boy called Simon Ledder had come up to him, accompanied by three or four henchmen, and started jeering about guardian angels. Matthew's disownment of a guardian angel went unheeded, and somehow a situation had been reached in which Simon proclaimed that if Matthew's guardian angel could guard him from his, Simon's, fists he was willing to believe in guardian angels, if not it proved that Matthew was a liar. Simon had then put his postulate to a practical test by landing Matthew a punch in the face which had knocked him down. Matthew was not quite clear about the next minute or two. He admitted he might have been dazed. All he remembered was that he was on his feet again, and instead of facing Simon and his companions he found himself looking at Mr Slatson, the headmaster.

Mr Slatson very decently took the trouble to ring up at dinner-time, and inquire about Matthew. I was able to tell him that he seemed quite himself, though he did not look pretty.

'I'm sorry it happened,' Mr Slatson said. 'The provocation was all on the other boy's part. We've settled that, and I don't think he'll try it again. A curious incident. I happened to see it though I was too far off to interfere. When the boy had knocked Matthew down he waited for him to get up again, with the obvious intention of following it up. But, when Matthew did get up, instead of stepping forward he took a pace back, so did his companions, they stared for a moment and then all turned and ran away. I asked the ring-leader what had happened. All he could tell me was that Matthew "looked so fierce". Odd that, but I think it means there'll be no more trouble of the kind. By the way . . .' And he went on to congratulate us, though with some detectably puzzled undertones, on Matthew's natatory and artistic achievements.

Polly was interested in Matthew's appearance.

'Can you see out of it?' she wanted to know.

'Yes,' Matthew said shortly.

'It does look funny,' she told him. 'Twinklehooves nearly lost his eye once,' she added, reminiscently.

'Got kicked by a ballet dancer?' suggested Matthew.

'No. It was in the book before that – when he was a hunting pony,' Polly explained. She paused. 'Did Chocky do it?' she asked innocently.

'Now then. Break it up,' I told them. 'Matthew, what did Miss Soames say about "Homeward". Was she pleased to see it in the papers?'

Matthew shook his head.

'I haven't seen her yet. We didn't have Art today,' he said.

'Miss Pinkser from our school saw it,' Polly put in. '*She* thought it was lousy.'

'Really, Polly, what an expression,' Mary protested. 'I'm sure Miss Pinkser didn't say anything of the kind.'

'I didn't say she said it. But she *thought* it. You could

tell. . . . She wanted to know if Matthew had something called stig – stigmatics, or something, and whether he wears glasses. And I told her no, he didn't need them because it wasn't really his picture, anyway.'

I exchanged glances with Mary.

'Oh dear, what have you started now, I wonder?' she said, with a sigh.

'Well, it's true,' Polly protested.

'It isn't,' said Matthew. 'It *is* my picture. Miss Soames watched me do it.'

Polly sniffed.

When we had got rid of them I gave Mary my news of the day. Landis had rung me up in the morning. He had, he told me, managed to see Sir William who seemed quite hopefully interested by his account of Matthew. Sir William's time was, of course, rather closely booked, but he had suggested that I ring up his secretary, and see if an appointment could be arranged.

So I did that. Sir William's secretary also told me that Sir William was very much booked-up, but she would see. There was a sound of riffling papers, then, on a gracious note, she informed me that I was fortunate; there had been a cancellation, two o'clock Friday afternoon if I cared to take it, otherwise it might be a matter of weeks.

Mary hesitated. She seemed, during the last two or three days, to have lost the fine edge of her antipathy to Chocky; also, I fancy, she had an instinctive reluctance to entrusting Matthew in other hands, as if, like the beginning of schooldays, it marked the end of a phase. But her commonsense asserted itself. We arranged that Matthew should come up on Friday, and I would escort him to Harley Street.

On Wednesday I had an uninterrupted day. Mary was obliged to fend off only two personal callers and two telephone callers wanting Matthew, and his school gave a short dismissal to a would-be interviewer from the

Psychic Observer. Matthew himself, however, had a brush with Mr Caffer.

It arose, apparently, from Mr Caffer's assertion during a physics lesson that the speed of light was the limit; nothing, he dogmatically stated, could travel faster than light.

Matthew put up his hand. Mr Caffer looked at him.

'Oh,' he said, 'I might have expected it. Well, young Gore, what is it you know that Einstein didn't?'

Matthew, already regretting his impulse, said:

'It doesn't matter, sir.'

'But it does,' said Mr Caffer. 'Any challenge to Einstein is most important. Let's have it.'

'Well, sir, it's just that the speed of light is only the limit of *physical* speed.'

'Indeed. And perhaps you can tell us what travels faster?'

'Thought, sir,' said Matthew.

Mr Caffer regarded him.

'Thought, Gore, is a physical process. It involves neural messages, synapses, chemical changes in the cells among other things. All that takes time. It can be measured in micro-seconds. I assure you you will find it is considerably slower than light. If it weren't, many nasty road accidents could be avoided.'

'But . . .'

'But what, Gore?'

'Well, sir. Perhaps I wasn't really meaning thought. I was meaning mind.'

'Oh, were you? Psychology isn't really my subject. Perhaps you will explain to us.'

'Well, sir, if you can sort of throw your mind – '

' "Sort of throw – "? would "project" be the word?'

'Yes, sir. If you can project your mind, space and time sort of don't count. You can go right through them at once.'

'I see. A most interesting proposition. Perhaps you yourself can perform this feat?'

'No, sir, I can't – ' Matthew dried up, suddenly.

'But you know someone who can? I'm sure we should find it most instructive if you were to bring him along some time.' He gazed sadly at Matthew, and shook his head. Matthew dropped his eyes to his desk top.

'Well,' said Mr Caffer, addressing himself to the class once more, 'now that we have established that nothing in the universe – with the possible exception of Matthew Gore's mind – can exceed the speed of light, let us return to our lesson . . .'

On Friday I met Matthew off the train at Waterloo. We had lunch and arrived in Harley Street with five minutes to spare.

Sir William Thorbe turned out to be a tall, clean-shaven man with a rather high-bridged nose, fine hair just greying, and a pair of dark, perceptive eyes under thick eyebrows. In other circumstances I should have thought him a barrister rather than a medical man, his air, appearance, and carriage gave a first misleading impression of familiarity which I later ascribed to his resemblance to the Duke of Wellington.

I introduced Matthew, exchanged a few words, and was then shown out to wait.

'How long?' I asked the secretary.

'Two hours is the minimum with a new patient,' she told me. 'I suggest you come back at half-past four. We'll look after your boy if he's through before that.'

I went back to the office, and returned on time. It was after five before Matthew emerged. He looked at the clock.

'Gosh,' he said. 'I thought it was only about half an hour.'

The secretary bustled up.

'Sir William asks me to make his apologies for not seeing you now. He has an urgent consultation to attend. He will be writing to you in a day or two,' she said, and we were shown out.

'What happened?' I asked Matthew when we were in the train.

'He asked me some questions. He didn't seem at all surprised about Chocky,' he said, and added: 'Then we listened to records.'

'Oh. He runs a discothèque?' I inquired.

'Not that sort of record. It was all soft and quiet – musical kind of music. It just went on while he asked the questions. And then when it stopped he took another record out of a cupboard and asked me if I had ever seen one like that. I said no, because it was a funny looking record with black and white patterns all over it. So he moved a chair and said: "Sit here where you can see it," and he put it on the record-player.

'It made a queer humming noise, not real music at all, though it went up and down a bit. Then there was another humming noise, a sort of sharper one. It came in on top of the other humming, and went up and down, too. I watched the record going round, and all the pattern seemed to be running into the middle – a bit like bath-water running out of the plug-hole, only not quite because it didn't go down, it just ran into itself and disappeared to nowhere, and kept on doing it. It was funny watching it because I began to feel as if the whole room was turning round, and I was falling off the chair. Then, quite suddenly it was all right again and there was an ordinary record with ordinary music coming out of it.

'Well, then Sir William gave me an orange drink, and asked some more questions, and after a bit he said that'd be all for today, and good-bye, and I came out.'

I duly reported to Mary.

'Oh,' she said. 'Hypnosis. I don't think I like that very much.'

'No,' I agreed. 'But I suppose he'd use whatever method seemed appropriate. Matthew can be pretty cagey about Chocky. I know he opened up with Landis, but that was exceptional. If Sir William was having to fight for every answer he may well have felt that hypnosis would make it easier for both of them.'

'M'm,' said Mary, 'well, all we can do now is to wait for his report.'

The next morning, Saturday, Matthew came down to breakfast looking tired. He was low-spirited, too, and listless. He refused Polly's invitation to dispute with such gloomy distaste that Mary dropped on her heavily, and shut her up.

'Are you not feeling well?' she demanded of Matthew, who was toying uninterestedly with his cornflakes.

'I'm all right,' he said.

'You're sure?'

'Yes.' He told her.

Mary regarded him, and tried again.

'It's not anything to do with yesterday? Did that man do something that upset you?'

'No,' Matthew shook his head. 'I'm all right,' he repeated, and attacked his cornflakes as if in demonstration. He got them down as if every leaf were threatening to choke him.

I watched him closely, and had a strong impression he was on the verge of tears.

'Look, old man. I've got to go down to Chichester today. Would you like to come along?' I suggested.

He shook his head again.

'No, thank you, Daddy. I'd rather – Mummy, can I just have some sandwiches, please?'

Mary looked at me in question. I nodded.

'All right, darling. I'll cut you some after breakfast,' she said.

Matthew ate a little more, and then disappeared upstairs.

'Twinklehooves went off his feed when his friend Stareyes died. It was very sad,' Polly remarked.

'You go up and brush that hair. It's disgusting,' Mary told her.

When we were alone she said:

'I'm sure it's something that man told him yesterday.'

'Could be,' I admitted. 'But I don't think so. He wasn't at all upset yesterday evening. Anyway, if he wants to get away by himself, I think we ought to let him.'

When I went out to get the car I found Matthew strapping a sketching-block, his paint-box, and a packet of sandwiches on to the carrier of his bicycle. I hoped the sandwiches would survive it.

'Go carefully. Remember it's Saturday,' I told him.

He did not come back until six o'clock, and went straight up to his room. At dinner he was still up there. I inquired.

'He says he doesn't want any,' Mary told me. 'He's just lying on his bed staring at the ceiling. I'm sure he must be sickening for something.'

I went up to see. Matthew was, as Mary had said, lying on his bed. He looked very tired.

'Feeling played out, old man?' I asked him. 'Why don't you get right into bed? I'll bring you something on a tray.'

He shook his head.

'No thanks, Daddy. I don't want anything.'

'You ought to have something, you know.'

He shook his head again.

I looked round the room. There were four pictures I had not seen before. All landscapes. Two propped up on the mantel shelf, two on the chest of drawers.

'Did you do these today? May I look?' I asked.

I moved closer to them. One I recognized immediately, a view across Docksham Great Pond, another included a part of the pond in one corner, the third was taken from a higher point looking across a village to the Downs beyond, the fourth was like nothing I had ever seen.

It was a view across a plain. As a background a line of rounded, ancient-looking hills, topped here and there by squat, domed towers, was set against a cloudless blue sky. In the middle-ground, to the right of centre, stood something like a very large cairn. It had the shape, though not the regularity of a heightened pyramid, nor were the stones – if stones they were – fitted together; rather they seemed, as far as one could tell from the drawing, to be boulders piled up. It could scarcely have been called a building, yet it quite certainly was not a natural formation. In the foreground were rows of things precisely spaced and arranged in curving lines – I say 'things' because it was impossible to make out what they were; they could have been bulbous succulent plants, or haycocks, or, perhaps even, huts, there was no telling, and to make their shape more difficult to determine, each appeared to throw two shadows. From the left of the picture a wide, cleared strip ran straight as a ruler's edge to the foot of the cairn, where it changed direction towards a bank of haze at the foot of the mountains. It was a depressing vista, all except the blue of the sky, in unrelieved browns, reds, greys, filled with a sense of aridity, and the feeling of intolerable heat.

I was still looking at the thing, bewildered, when there was a gulp from the bed behind me. Matthew said, with difficulty:

'They're the last pictures, Daddy.'

I turned round. His eyes were screwed up, but tears were trickling out of them. I sat down on the bed beside him and took his hand.

'Matthew, boy, tell me. Tell me what the trouble is.'

Matthew sniffed, choked, and then stammered out:

'It's Chocky, Daddy. She's going away – for ever . . .'

I heard Mary's feet on the stairs, crossed swiftly to the door, and closed it behind me.

'What is it? Is he ill?' she asked.

I took her arm and moved away from the door.

'No. He'll be all right,' I told her, leading her back to the stairs.

'But what is the matter?' she insisted.

I shook my head. When we were down in the hall, safely out of earshot of Matthew's room I told her.

'It's Chocky. Apparently she's leaving – clearing out.'

'Well, thank goodness for that,' Mary said.

117

'Maybe, but don't let him see you think that.'

Mary considered.

'I'd better take him up a tray.'

'No. Leave him alone.'

'But the poor boy must eat.'

'I think he's – well, saying good-bye to her – and finding it difficult and painful,' I said.

She looked at me uncertainly, with a puzzled frown.

'But, David, you're talking as if – I mean, Chocky isn't *real*.'

'To Matthew she is. And he's taking it hard.'

'All the same, I think he ought to have some food.'

I have been astonished before, and doubtless shall be again, how the kindliest and most sympathetic of women can pettify and downgrade the searing anguishes of childhood.

'Later on, perhaps,' I said. 'But not now.'

Throughout the meal Polly chattered constantly and boringly of ponies. When we had got rid of her Mary asked:

'I've been thinking. Do you think it's something that man did?'

'What man?'

'That Sir William Something, of course,' she said, impatiently. 'After all he did hypnotize Matthew. People can be made to do all kinds of things through hypnotic suggestion. Suppose he said to Matthew, when he was in a trance: "Tomorrow you friend Chocky is going to tell you she is going away. You are going to be very sorry to say good-bye to her, but you will. Then she will leave you,

and gradually you will forget all about her" – something like that. I don't know much about it, but isn't it possible that a suggestion of that kind might cure him, and clear up the whole thing?'

' "Cure him"?' I said.

'Well, I mean ...'

'You mean you've gone back to thinking Chocky is an illusion?'

'Not exactly an illusion . . .'

'Really, darling – after the swimming, after watching him at his painting last week-end, you can still think that . . .?'

'I can still hope that. At least it's less alarming than what your friend Landis talked about – possession. And this does seem to bear it out, doesn't it? I mean, he goes to this Sir William man, and the very next day he tells you that Chocky is going away . . .'

I had to admit that she had a point there. I wished I knew more about hypnosis in general, and Matthew's in particular. I also wished very much that, if Sir William could contrive to expel Chocky by hypnosis, he could have contrived to do it in some way that would have caused Matthew less distress.

In fact, I found myself displeased with Sir William. It began to look as if I had taken Matthew to him for a diagnosis – which I had not yet got – and possibly been given instead a treatment, which I had not, at this stage, requested. The more I considered it, the more unsatisfactory, not to say high-handed, it seemed.

On our way to bed we looked into Matthew's room in case he were feeling hungry now. There was no sound except his regular breathing, so we shut the door quietly and went away.

The next morning, Sunday, we let him sleep on. He emerged about ten o'clock looking dazed with sleep, his eyes pink about the rims, his manner distrait, but with his appetite hugely restored.

About half past eleven a large American car with a front like a juke-box turned into the drive. Matthew came thundering down the stairs.

'It's Auntie Janet, Daddy. I'm off,' he said, breathlessly, and shot down the passage to the back door.

We had a trying day. Rather like a reception without the guest of honour – or, perhaps, a freak-show without the freak. Matthew had been wise. There was a lot of discussion, mostly one-sided, on the viability of guardian

angels, and a lengthy disquisition, with illustrative anec-
dotes, on the characteristics of an artist in the family,
presenting almost all of them as undesirable, if not
actually disruptive.

I do not know when Matthew returned. He must have
come in, burgled the larder, and crept upstairs while we
were talking. After they had gone I went up to his room.
He was sitting looking out of the open window at the
sinking sun.

'You'll have to face her sooner or later,' I told him. 'But
I must say today was not the day. They were most
disappointed not to see you.'

Matthew managed a grin.

I looked round. The four paintings were propped up
again on display. I commented favourably on the views of
Docksham Pond. When I came to the last picture I hesitated, wondering whether to ignore it. I decided not to.

'Wherever is that supposed to be?' I inquired.

Matthew turned his head to look at it.

'That's where Chocky lives,' he said, and paused. Then
he added. 'It's a horrid place, isn't it? That's why she
thinks this world is so beautiful.'

'Not at all an attractive spot,' I agreed. 'It looks terribly
hot there.'

'Oh, it is in the daytime. That fuzzy bit at the back is
vapour coming off a lake.'

I pointed to the great cairn.

'What is that thing?'

'I don't know, really,' Matthew admitted. 'Sometimes
she seems to mean a building, and sometimes it comes like
a lot of buildings, more like a town. It's a bit difficult
without words when there isn't anything the same here.'

That, I felt, must considerably understate the per-
plexities of mentally conveying an alien concept.

'And these lumps?' I pointed to the rows of symmetric-
ally spaced mounds.

'Things that grow there,' was all he could tell me.

'Where is it?' I asked.

Matthew shook his head.

'We still couldn't find out – or where our world is, either,' he said.

I noted his use of the past tense, and looked at the picture again. The harsh monotony of the colouring, and the feeling of arid heat struck me once more.

'You know, if I were you I'd keep it out of sight when you're not here. I don't think Mummy would like it very much.'

Matthew nodded. 'That's what I thought. So I put it away today.'

There was a pause. We looked out of the window at the red arc of sun fretted by the treetops as it set. I asked him:

'Has she gone, Matthew?'

'Yes, Daddy.'

We were silent while the last rim of the sun sank down and disappeared. Matthew sniffed. His eyes filled with tears.

'Oh, Daddy. . . . It's like losing part of me . . .'

Matthew was subdued, and perhaps a little pale the next morning, but he went off resolutely enough to school. He came back looking tired, but as the week went by he improved daily. By the end of it he seemed more like his normal self again. We were relieved; for the same reasons, but on different premises.

'Well, thank goodness that's over,' Mary said to me on Friday evening. 'It looks as if Sir William Thing was right after all.'

'Thorbe,' I said.

'Well, Thing or Thorbe. The point is that he told you that it was just a phase, that Matthew had built up an elaborate fantasy system, that it was nothing very unusual at his age, and there was nothing for us to worry about – unless it were to become persistent. He thought that unlikely. In his opinion the fantasy would break up of itself, and disperse – probably quite soon. And that's exactly what's happened.'

'Yes,' I agreed. It was the simplest way, and, after all, what did it matter now if Thorbe had been right off the beam. Chocky was, in one way or another, gone.

Nevertheless when I had received his letter on the Tuesday, I had found it exceedingly hard to take. The swimming he dealt with by explaining that Matthew had in fact learned to swim some time before, but a deep-seated fear of the water had caused him to suppress the ability, thus rendering it merely latent. This dormancy had persisted until the shock of the emergency caused by his sudden immersion had broken down the mental block, and allowed the latent ability to manifest itself. Naturally, his conscious mind remained ignorant of the inhibiting block, and had attributed the ability to an extraneous influence.

Rather similarly with the pictures. Undoubtedly Matthew had in his subconscious mind a strong desire to paint. This had remained suppressed, quite possibly as a result of terror inspired in him by the sight of horrifying pictures at an early age. Only when his present fantasy had grown potent enough to affect both his conscious and his subconscious minds, forming, as it were, a bridge between them, had the urge to paint become liberated and capable of expressing itself in action.

There were explanations of the car incident, and others, along roughly the same lines. And though much of what I considered worthy of attention had been ignored I had little doubt he could have explained that away, too, upon request.

It was not only one of the most disappointing letters I have ever waited for; it was insulting in the naïve smoothness of its elucidations, and patronizing in its reassurances. I was furious that Mary could take it at face value; still more furious that events appeared to justify her in doing so. I realized that I had expected a lot from Thorbe: I felt that all I had got was a brush-off, and a let-down.

And yet the fellow had been right. ... The Chocky-presence *had* dispersed, as he put it. The Chocky-trauma *seemed* to be mending – though I felt less sure of that . . .

So I contented myself with a simple 'yes', and let Mary go on telling me in as sympathetic a way as possible how wrong I had been to perceive subtle complexities in what had, after all, turned out to be just a rather more developed, and certainly more troublesome, version of Piff. It did her quite a lot of good. So, fair enough.

I had always thought from the evidence of newspapers that Societies, particularly Royal ones of this and that, must spend some considerable time in serious conclave checking upon the standing of commenders, the credibility of eye-witnesses, the authenticity of the represented circumstances, and the moral integrity of everyone connected with the event before they would sanction the presentation of one of their precious awards. All this, I reckoned, might take an authenticating minimum of six months, whereafter one might expect that sooner or later the recipient would be summoned to a presentation in the presence of the Council, this may be the procedure in some Societies: it is not so, however, with the Royal Swimming Society.

Their tribute arrived unheralded, and prosaically by registered post on the Monday morning addressed to Mr Matthew Gore. Unfortunately I was unable to intercept it. Mary signed for it, and when Matthew and I arrived in the dining-room together it was lying beside his plate.

Matthew glanced at the envelope, stiffened and sat quite still looking at it for some moments. Then he turned to his cornflakes. I tried to catch Mary's eye, but in vain. She leant forward.

'Aren't you going to open it?' she asked, encouragingly.

Matthew looked at it again. His eyes roved round the table, looking for an escape. They encountered his mother's expectant expression. Very reluctantly he picked up his knife and slit the envelope. A small red, leather-covered box slid out. He hesitated again. Slowly he picked it up, and opened it. For some seconds he was motionless, gazing at the golden disc gleaming in its bed of blue velvet. Then:

'I don't want it,' he blurted.

This time I did manage to catch Mary's eye, and gave a slight shake of my head.

Matthew's lower lip came out a little. It shook slightly.

'It's not fair,' he said. 'It's Chocky's – *she* saved me *and* Polly. . . . It's not *true*, Daddy . . .'

He went on looking at the medal, head down. I felt a poignant memory of those desolate patches of disillusion which are the shocks of growing up. The discovery that one lived in a world which could pay honour where honour was not due, was just such a one. The values were rocked, the dependable was suddenly flimsy, the solid became hollow, gold turned to brass, there was no integrity anywhere . . .

Matthew got up, and ran blindly out of the room. The medal, gaudily shining in its case, lay on the table.

I picked it up. The obverse was a trifle florid. The Society's name in full ran round the edge, then there was a band of involved ornament with a suggestion of debased art-nouveau, in the centre a boy and a girl standing hand in hand looking at half a sun which radiated vigorously, presumably in the act of rising.

I turned it over. The reverse was plainer. Simply an inscription within a circular wreath of laurel leaves. Above:

AWARDED TO

then, engraved in a different type-face:

MATTHEW GORE

and, finally, the all-purpose laudation:

FOR A VALOROUS DEED

I handed it to Mary.

She examined it thoughtfully for some moments, and then put it back in its case.

'It's a shame he's taken it like that,' she said.

I picked up the case, and slipped it into my pocket.

'It's unfortunate it arrived just now,' I agreed. 'I'll keep it for him until later on.'

Mary looked as if she might demur, but at that moment Polly arrived babbling, and anxious not to be late for school.

I looked upstairs before I left, but Matthew had already gone – and left his books of homework lying on the table . . .

He turned up again about half past six, just after I had got home.

'Oh,' I said, 'and where have you been all day?'

'Walking,' he told me.

I shook my head.

'It won't do, Matthew, you know. You can't just go cutting school like that.'

'I know,' he agreed.

The rest of our conversation was unspoken. We understood one another well enough.

Ten

The rest of the week went uneventfully, until Friday. I had to work late that evening, and had dinner in London. At almost ten o'clock I arrived home to find Mary on the telephone. She finished her call just as I came into the room, and pressed the rest without putting the receiver on it.

'Matthew's not back,' she said. 'I'm ringing the hospitals.'

She consulted a list and began to dial again. After two or three more calls she came to the end of her list, and laid the receiver in its rest. I had got out the whisky.

'Drink this. It'll do you good,' I told her.

She took it, gratefully.

'You've tried the police?'

'Yes. I called the school first. He left there at the usual time all right. So then I tried the police, and gave them particulars. They've promised to ring us if they have any news.' She took a drink of whisky. 'Oh, David. Thank goodness you're back. I'd got to imagining all sorts of things. ... I hoped everything would be all right once that Chocky business was over. But he's gone all closed in. ... He doesn't *say* anything – not to me. ... And then going off like he did on Monday. ... You don't think ...?'

I sat down beside her, and took her hand.

'Of course I don't, And you mustn't either.'

'He's kept everything so bottled up ...'

'It did come as a shock to him. Whatever Chocky was he'd got used to having her around. Suddenly losing her upset him – knocked the bottom out of things for him. It needed some adjustment – but he's making it all right ...'

'You really think that? You're not just saying it . . .?'

'Of course I do, darling. I'm perfectly certain that if he were going to do anything silly he'd have done it a fortnight ago, and he wasn't near that even then – he was distressed and pretty wretched, poor boy. But nothing of that kind ever entered his head. I'm sure of it.'

Mary sighed.

'I hope you're right – yes, I'm sure you are. But that makes it all the more mysterious. He must know how we'll feel. He's not an insensitive boy . . .'

'Yes,' I agreed. 'That's what's worrying me most . . .'

Neither of us slept much that night.

I rang the police the next morning. They were sympathetic, doing all they could, but had no news.

The gloominess of the breakfast table subdued even Polly. We questioned her though without much hope. Matthew no longer confided in her, but there was just the chance that he might have let something slip. Apparently he had not – at least nothing that Polly could remember. We relapsed into our gloomy silence. Polly emerged from hers to say:

'I expect Matthew's been kidnapped. You'll probably get a note wanting an enormous ransom.'

'Not very likely,' I told her. 'We don't keep enormous ransoms round here.'

Silence closed down again. After a time Polly found it irksome. She fidgeted. Presently she felt impelled to make conversation. She observed:

'When Twinklehooves was kidnapped they tried to turn him into a pit pony.'

'Shut up,' I told her. 'Either shut up, or go away.'

She regarded me with hurt reproof, but decided to go away, in a huff.

'What about the Sunday papers? They were anxious enough to interview him before,' Mary suggested.

'You know what that means. "Child Artist Vanishes." "Guardian Angel Hero Missing", et cetera.'

'What's that matter if it helps to find him?'

'All right,' I told her. 'I'll try.'

There was no news that day.

At ten o'clock on Sunday morning the phone rang. I grabbed it.

'Mr Gore?'

'Yes.'

'My name is Bollot. You don't know me, but my boy goes to the same school as yours. We've just been reading in the paper about it. Shocking business. Very sorry to hear it. No news yet, I suppose?'

'No.'

'Well, look here, the point is my Lawrence says he saw your Matthew on Friday. He noticed him talking to a man with a big car – a Mercedes, he thinks – a little way down the road from the school. He has an idea they were arguing about something. Then your Matthew got into the car with the man, and it drove off.'

'Thanks, Mr Bollot. Thanks very much. I'll let the police know at once.'

'Oh, is that really – ? Yes, I suppose it is. Well, I hope they find him quickly for you.'

But they did not.

The Monday papers took it up. The BBC included it in their local news bulletin. The phone seemed scarcely to stop ringing. But it brought no news of Matthew . . .

That was a dreadful week. What can one do in the face of utter blankness? There was no corroboration of the Bollot boy's story, but he stuck to it with unshakeable conviction. An inquiry at the school failed to discover any other boy who had accepted a lift that evening. So, apparently, it had been Matthew . . .

But why? What possible reason? Even threats, a demand for ransom would have been more bearable than this silent vanishing into utter nothingness which left our imaginations roving horridly at large. I could feel the tension in Mary growing tighter every day, and dreaded the moment when it should break . . .

The week seemed endless. The week-end that followed it, longer still, but then:

At about half past eight o'clock on the following Tuesday morning a small boy paused on the pavement edge of a busy crossing in Birmingham, and watched the policeman directing the traffic. When that ahead of him was held up he crossed to the middle of the road, stationed himself alongside the policeman, waiting patiently to be attended to. Presently, his traffic safely on course for the moment, the policeman bent down.

'Hullo, Sonny, and what's your trouble?' he inquired.

'Please, sir,' said the boy, 'I'm afraid I'm sort of lost. And it's difficult because I haven't any money to get home with.'

The policeman shook his head.

'That's bad,' he said, sympathetically. 'And where would home be?'

'Hindmere,' the boy told him.

The policeman stiffened, and looked at him with sudden interest.

'And what's your name?' he asked, carefully.

'Matthew,' said Matthew. 'Matthew Gore.'

'Is it, begod!' said the policeman. 'Now you stand just where you are, Matthew. Don't you move an inch.'

He took a microphone out of his breast-pocket, pressed a switch, and spoke into it.

A squad car drew up beside them a couple of minutes later.

'That's service for you. Come to take you home. Hop in now,' the policeman told him.

'Thank you very much, sir,' said Matthew, with his customary respect for the police.

They brought him home about six o'clock that evening. Mary had rung me up, and I was there to greet him, so, by request, was Dr Aycott.

Matthew seemed to be on very good terms with his

escort. He invited them in, but they spoke of duty. Matthew thanked them, we thanked them, and they drove off, narrowly missing a car that was turning in. It's driver introduced himself as Dr Prost, police surgeon, and we all went inside.

We had drinks, and after ten minutes or so Dr Prost spoke quietly to Mary. She took Matthew off in spite of his protests that the police had already given him a super tea.

'Well, first of all,' said Dr Prost as the door closed behind them, 'you can put your mind at rest. The boy has come to no harm, no harm at all as far as we can tell. Furthermore, he has not even been frightened. It is quite the most considerate kidnapping that I have ever heard of. I see no reason at all for you to fear any ill-effects either physical, or mental. He seems to me to be in A1 condition.

'But, having said that, there are one or two things I think I ought to mention, which is why I wanted you, Dr Aycott, to come along. In the first place, he has had a number of injections. A dozen or more, in both arms. We have no idea at all what was injected. Whatever it was, it appears to have had no after effects, depressant, or otherwise. He makes no complaints of lassitude, or any abnormal condition. In fact he appears to be in excellent spirits. Nevertheless, since there have been these injections we feel that it would be wise to keep a careful eye on him for any delayed reactions. We have no reason to expect them, but we thought it as well, Doctor, that you should be informed of the possibility.'

Dr Aycott nodded. Dr Prost went on:

'The second thing is rather curious. Matthew is quite convinced that he has been in a car accident, and that his leg was fractured. Specifically, his right leg. He says that it was in plaster, and that the people "at the hospital" gave him a new treatment which made it mend very quickly. In our examination we found slight abrasions, and a skin condition consistent with the use of a plaster cast on the limb. Naturally, we X-rayed. There was no sign of a break.'

He paused, frowned into his whisky, and tossed it off. He went on:

'He seems to have been treated very well. Everybody at "the hospital" was friendly and reassuring. The whole, thing has the appearance of an elaborate hoax deliberately contrived to be as unalarming to him as possible. In fact it seems never to have occurred to him that he had been kidnapped. The only two jarring elements that puzzled him were, first, why you and his mother did not go to see him, or answer when he wrote to you, and, second, the way he was dumped in Birmingham.

'It looks to us very much as if somebody wanted him out of the way for ten days, or so.' He turned a penetrating look on me. 'If you know, or suspect, anybody who could have an interest in doing that, I think you'd be well advised to tell the police.'

I shook my head.

'I can't think of any conceivable reason for anyone to want to do such a thing. There's no sense in it,' I said.

He shrugged.

'Well, if you can think of any other explanation –' he said, and left it in the air, not looking entirely convinced.

He and Dr Aycott conferred briefly, and left together a few minutes later, Dr Aycott promising to look in the next day.

I found Matthew, Mary, and Polly in the kitchen. The police super tea had left him with some appetite still. I sat down and lit a cigarette.

'Well, now, suppose you tell us all about it, Matthew,' I suggested.

'Oh dear. Again?' said Matthew.

'You haven't told *us* yet,' I pointed out.

Matthew took a deep breath.

'Well, I was just coming home from school, and this car passed me and stopped a little way in front. And a man got out and looked up and down the road in a lost sort of way,' he began.

The man looked at Matthew, appeared to be about to

speak, but hesitated, then just as Matthew was passing him he said:

'Excuse me, but I wonder if you could help us. We're looking for Densham Road, but none of the roads here seem to have any names.'

'Yes,' said Matthew. 'You turn right at the next corner, then the second on the left. That's Old Lane, only when you get over the crossroads it's called Densham Road.'

'Thank you. That's very clear,' said the man, and turned to the car. Then, on an afterthought, he turned back.

'I suppose you couldn't tell us which side of it to look for a house called Poyntings? A Mr Gore lives there.'

It was as easy as that. Of course Matthew accepted the offer of a lift home. He did not know anything else until he woke up in 'the hospital'.

'What made you think it was a hospital?' Mary asked.

'It looked like one – well, the way I think hospitals look,' said Matthew. 'I was in a white bed, and the room was all white and bare and terribly clean. And there was a nurse; she was frightfully clean, too.'

He had discovered that he couldn't move his leg. The nurse told him not to try because it had been broken, and asked him if it hurt. He told her it didn't a bit. She had said 'good', and that was because he had been injected with a new 'anti-something' drug that stopped the pain, and not to worry because they were using a wonderful new process which healed bones, particularly young ones, very quickly.

There had been two or three doctors – well, they wore white coats like doctors on television, anyway – and they were very friendly and cheerful. There was rather a lot of injecting. He hadn't liked that at first, but didn't mind it much after the first two or three times. Anyway, it was worth it because the leg hadn't hurt at all.

Sometimes it had been a bit boring, but they gave him some books. They hadn't a radio to spare, they told him, but they had let him have a record-player with lots of records. The food was jolly good.

His chief disappointment was that we had not come to see him.

'Of course we'd have come if we could, but we'd no idea where you were,' Mary told him.

'They said they'd told you. And I wrote you two letters with the address at the top,' Matthew protested.

'I'm afraid nobody did tell us. And we never got your letters, either,' I said. 'What was the address?'

'Aptford House, Wonersh, near Guildford,' he told me promptly.

'You've told the police that?'

'Yes.'

He went on. Apparently he'd seen nothing of the place save the room he had been kept in. The view from its window had been undistinguished, a meadow in the foreground, bounded by a hedge with tall trees in it. Sometime the day before yesterday they had taken off the cast, examined his leg, told him it had mended perfectly, and would be as good as ever, and that he'd be able to go home the next day.

Actually they had started in the dark – he did not know the time because there was no clock in the room. He had said good-bye to the nurse. One of the doctors – not in a white coat this time – had taken him downstairs to where there was a big car waiting in front of the house. When they got in the back the doctor said they'd leave the light on, but had better have the blinds down so as not to dazzle the driver. After they'd started the doctor produced a pack of cards and did some tricks with them. Then the doctor brought out a couple of vacuum flasks, coffee in one for himself, cocoa in the other for Matthew. Shortly after that Matthew had fallen asleep.

He had woken up feeling rather cold. The car had stopped, and there was daylight outside. When he sat up he discovered that not only was he all alone, but he was in a different car which was parked in an utterly unfamiliar street. It was very bewildering. He got out of the car. There were few people walking along the street, but they looked busily on their way somewhere, and took no notice of him. At the end of the street he saw its name on the wall of the building. He didn't remember what it was, but above it he read 'City of Birmingham', which puzzled him greatly. He was now facing a bigger, busier street, with a small café just opposite. He became aware that he was hungry, but when he felt in his pocket he found he'd no money. After that, the only thing to do had seemed to be to find a policeman, and put his problems to him.

'A very sensible thing to do, too,' I told him.

'Yes . . .' said Matthew, doubtfully. 'But they kept on asking so many questions.'

'And they brought you all the way home in a Z car, free?' Polly asked.

'Well, three cars,' Matthew told her. 'There was one to the Birmingham police station where they asked a lot of questions, then one to the Hindmere police station, where they gave me that super tea, and asked all the same questions over again. And then one here.'

'Gosh, you are lucky,' said Polly enviously. 'When Twinklehooves was kidnapped they had to hire a horse-box to bring *him* home. It was very expensive.'

'Kidnapped . . .' Matthew repeated. 'But. . . .' He broke off, and became very thoughtful. He turned to me.

'Was *I* kidnapped, Daddy?'

'It looks very much like it.' I told him.

'But – but. . . . But they were *kind* people, nice people. They got me better. They weren't a bit like kidnappers. . . .' He lapsed into thought again, and emerged from it to ask: 'Do you mean it was all phoney – my leg wasn't broken at all?'

I nodded.

'I don't believe it. It had plaster on – and everything,' he protested. 'Anyway, why? Why should anybody want to kidnap *me*?' He checked, and then asked. 'Did you have to pay a lot of money, Daddy?'

I shook my head again.

'No. Nothing at all,' I assured him.

'Then it can't have been kidnapping,' asserted Matthew.

'You must be tired out,' Mary put in. 'Give me a kiss. Then run along upstairs, both of you. Daddy and I will come up and see you when you're in bed, Matthew.'

The door closed behind him. Mary looked at me, her eyes brimming. Then she laid her head on her arms on the table and – for the first time since Matthew had disappeared – she let herself cry . . .

Eleven

That was Tuesday.

On Wednesday Dr Aycott looked in as he had promised. He gave Matthew a very thorough examination with so satisfactory a result that he saw no reason why Matthew should not go to school the following day.

On Wednesday, also, Mary felt it incumbent upon her to ring up her sister Janet and inform her that Matthew was now restored to us in perfect health, and then had to spend some time explaining that his health was not perhaps quite perfect enough to withstand a family invasion the next week-end.

On Thursday Matthew went to school and returned a bit above himself on discovering that he had been a figure of national interest while at the same time feeling somewhat inadequate in not having a more exciting tale to tell.

By Friday everything was back to normal.

That evening Mary, feeling tired, went upstairs soon after ten. I stayed down. I had brought home some work, and thought I would clear it off to leave the week-end free.

About half past eleven there was a tap on the door. Matthew's head appeared, and looked cautiously round.

'Has Mummy gone to bed?' he inquired.

I nodded.

'Some time ago. It's where you ought to be,' I told him.

'Good,' he said, and came in, carefully closing the door behind him. He was wearing his dressing-gown and bedroom slippers, and his hair was all on end. I wondered if he had been having a nightmare.

'What's the matter?' I asked.

He glanced back at the door as if to make sure it was closed.

'It's Chocky,' he told me.

My spirits sank a little.

'I thought she'd gone away – for good,' I said.

Matthew nodded.

'She did. But she's come back now. She says she wants me to tell you some things.'

I sighed. It had been a relief to think that we had finished with all that, but Matthew was looking very earnest and somewhat troubled. I took a cigarette, lit it, and leaned back.

'All right,' I said. 'I'm all attention. What things?'

But Matthew had become abstracted. He did not appear to hear. He noticed my expression though.

'Sorry, Daddy. Just a minute,' he said, and reverted to his look of abstraction. His changes of expression and the small movements of his head gave one a sensation of seeing one side of a televised conversation, with the sound cut off. It ended with him nodding and saying aloud: 'Okay. I'll try,' though rather doubtfully. Looking at me again he explained:

'Chocky says it'll take an awful long time if she has to tell me and then I have to tell you because sometimes I can't think of the right words for what she means; and sometimes they don't quite mean it when I can; if you see what I mean.'

'I think I do,' I told him. 'Lots of other people have difficulty over that at the best of times. And when it's a kind of translation, too, it must be quite hard work.'

'Yes, it is,' Matthew agreed, decidedly. 'So Chocky thinks it would be better if she talks to you herself.'

'Oh,' I said. 'Well – tell her to go ahead. What do I do?'

'No, not the way she talks to me. I don't understand why, but she says that only works with some people. It doesn't with you, so she wants to try and see if we can do it another way.'

'What other way?' I inquired.

'Well, me talking, but sort of letting her do it. . . . Like my hands and the painting,' he explained, not very adequately.

'Oh,' I said again, this time doubtfully. I was feeling at sea, unclear what was implied, uncertain whether it ought to be encouraged. 'I don't know. Do you think . . . ?'

'*I* don't know,' he said. 'But Chocky's pretty sure she can work it okay, so I expect she can. She's usually right about things like that.'

I was uneasy, with a feeling that I was being rushed into taking part in something suspiciously like a séance. I stalled.

'Look here,' I said. 'If this is going to take some time, don't you think it would be better if you were in bed. You'd keep warmer there.'

'All right,' agreed Matthew.

So we went up to his room. He got back to bed, and I sat down in a chair. I still had misgivings, a feeling that I ought not to be allowing this to go on – and a conviction that if Mary were here she would disapprove strongly – which was scarcely allayed by the hope that once Matthew was back in bed again he would fall asleep.

Matthew leant his head back on the pillow, and closed his eyes.

'I am going to think of nothing,' he said.

I hesitated. Then:

'Look here, Matthew. Don't you . . . ?' I began, and then broke off as his eyes reopened. They were not looking at me now, nor, seemingly, at anything else. His lips parted, came together two or three times without a sound, parted again, and his voice said:

'It is Chocky talking.'

There was no air of séance about it, nothing of the

medium about Matthew, no pallor, no change in his rate of breathing. Except for the unfocused look in his eyes he was apparently quite himself. The voice went on:

'I want to explain some things to you. It is not easy because I can use only Matthew's understanding, and only his' – there was a slight pause – 'vocabulary, which is simple, and not large, and has some meanings not clear in his mind.'

The voice was characteristically Matthew's, but the flatness of its delivery was certainly not. There was an impression of intended decisiveness blurred, and frustrated; an athlete condemned to take part in a sack-race. Unwillingly fascinated I said:

'Very well, I'll do my best to follow you.'

'I want to talk to you because I shall not come back again after this. You will be glad to hear this: the other part of his parent, I mean Mummy, I mean your wife, will be gladder because it is afraid of me and thinks I am bad for Matthew, which is a pity because I did not mean me, I mean you, I mean Matthew, any harm. Do you understand?'

'I think so,' I said, cautiously. 'But wouldn't it be best to tell me first who you are, what you are, why you are here at all?'

'I am an explorer, I mean scout, I mean missionary – no, I mean teacher. I am here to teach things.'

'Oh, are you? What sort of things?'

There was a pause, then:

'Matthew hasn't words for them – he doesn't understand them.'

'Not, perhaps, a very successful teacher?'

'Not yet. Matthew is too young. He can only think in too simple words for difficult ideas. If I think in maths, or physics, we do not meet. Even numbers are difficult. This is a good thing, I mean, lucky.'

I have quoted the above exchanges as closely as I can remember in order to give some idea of what I was up against, and to justify my use of editorial discretion from now on. A verbatim record would be impossible. The small-change words and usages came easily enough, but less familiar words brought hold-ups. There were detours in search of the right word, and others to establish the true significance of the approximate word that had been pressed into service, also several expeditions up cul-de-sacs where sheer inadequacy of vocabulary left us faced by a blank wall.

Add to that the necessity to wade through a morass of Matthew's favourite, and not very specific, adjectives: sort-of, kind-of, and I-mean, and the going became so intricate that it is quite necessary for me to edit ruthlessly in order to extract and attempt to convey Chocky's *intended* meaning – in so far as I could grasp it, which was not always.

I could perceive from the beginning that it was not going to be easy. The sight of Matthew lying there, quite expressionless as he spoke, his eyes with that unfocused stare, and his whole mien far more negative than that of a ventriloquist's dummy was too disturbing for me to give the words the full attention they needed.

I turned out the light as an aid to concentration – and in sneaking hope that without it he might fall asleep.

'All right. Go ahead,' I said into the darkness. 'You are a missionary – or a teacher – or an explorer. Where from?'

'Far away.'

'Far? How far?'

'I do not know. Many, many parsecs.'

'Oh,' I said.

'I was sent here to find out what kind of a planet this is.'

'Were you indeed. Why?'

'To see, in the first place, whether it would be useful to us. You see, we are a very old people compared with you, on a very old planet compared with yours. It has long been clear to us that if we are to survive we must colonize. But that is difficult. A ship that can travel only at the speed of light takes a very long time to get anywhere. One cannot send out ships on the chance of their finding a suitable planet. There are innumerable millions of planets. The chance of finding a suitable one is infinitesimal.

'So a scout – an explorer – is sent out in this way. Because mind has no mass it takes no time to travel. The scout makes his report. If he reports that it would be a suitable planet for a colony, other scouts are sent to check. If their reports are favourable, the astronomers go to work to locate the planet. If it is found to be within practicable range they may send a ship of colonists. But this is very rare. It has happened only four times in a thousand of your years. And only two colonies have been established.'

'I see. And when are we to expect a ship here?'

'Oh, this planet is not any use to us. Your planet is exceptional, and very beautiful, but it is much too cold for us, and there is a great deal too much water. There are plenty of reasons why it is quite impossible for us. I could tell that at once.'

'Then why stay here? Why not go and find a more suitable planet?'

Chocky went on, patiently:

'We are explorers. We are at present, as far as we know, the only explorers of the universe. For a long time we thought that ours was the only planet that could support life. Then we found others that could – a few. For still longer we thought we were unique – the only intelligent form of life – a single, freakish pinpoint of reason in a vast, adventitious cosmos – utterly lonely in the horrid wastes of space. ... Again we discovered we were mistaken ...

'But intelligent life is rare ... very rare indeed ... the rarest thing in creation ...

'But the most precious ...

'For intelligent life is the only thing that gives meaning

to the universe. It is a holy thing, to be fostered and treasured.

'Without it nothing begins, nothing ends, there can be nothing through all eternity but the mindless babblings of chaos . . .

'Therefore, the nurture of all intelligent forms is a sacred duty. Even the merest spark of reason must be fanned in the hope of a flame. Frustrated intelligence must have its bonds broken. Narrow-channelled intelligence must be given the power to widen out. High intelligence must be learned from. That is why I have stayed here.'

It took some time to get all that across. It seemed very high-minded, if a little high-flown. I asked:

'And into which of these categories do you consider the intelligent life of this planet to fall?'

The Chocky-Matthew voice answered that without hesitation.

'Narrow-channelled. It has recently managed to overcome some of its frustrations by its own efforts – which is hopefully good progress at your age. It is now in a groove of primitive technology.'

'It seems to us to be making progress pretty fast.'

'Yes. You have not done badly with electricity in a hundred years. And you did well with steam in quite a short time. But all that is so cumbersome, so inefficient. And your oil engines are just a deplorable perversion – dirty, noisy, poisonous, and the cars you drive with them are barbarous, dangerous . . .'

'Yes,' I interrupted. 'You mentioned that before, to Matthew. But we do have atomic power now.'

'Very crudely, yes. You are learning, slowly. But you still live in a finite, sun-based economy.'

'Sun-based?'

'Yes. Everything you are, and have, you owe to the radiations from your sun. Direct radiations you must have in order to keep your bodies alive, and to grow your food, and provide fresh water; and they could continue to sustain you for millions of years. But intelligence held at subsistence level cannot come to flower. To grow and expand it needs power.

'Recently you have learnt to exploit the stored-up energy of your sun – for that is what all your fuels are – and you call that progress. It is *not* progress. Progress is an advance towards an objective. What is your objective? You do not know, and since you do not know, you might as well be going round in a circle – which, indeed, is just what you are doing, for you are squandering your sources of power. And they are your capital: when they are spent you will be back where you were before you found them. This is not progress, it is profligacy.

'Your fuels, your capital, should certainly be used. Frozen power does no good to anyone. But *used*, not wasted. They should be invested, to produce greater power.

'It is true you have an elementary form of atomic power which you will no doubt improve. But that is almost your only investment for your future. Most of your power is being used to build machines to consume power faster and faster, while your sources of power remain finite. There can be only one end to that.'

'You have a point there,' I conceded. 'What, in your opinion, ought we to be doing?'

'You should be employing your resources, while you still have them, to tap and develop the use of a source of power which is *not* finite. Once you have access to an infinite supply of power you will have broken out of the closed circle of your solar-economy. You will no longer be isolated and condemned to eventual degeneration upon a wasting asset. You will become a part of the larger creation, for a source of infinite power is a source of infinite possibilities.'

'I see,' I said. 'At least, I think I see – dimly. What is this source of infinite power?'

'It is radiation – throughout the cosmos. It can be tapped and used.'

I thought. Then I said:

'It is a funny thing that in a world swarming with scientists nobody has suspected the existence of this source of power.'

'It is an equally funny thing that two hundred of your years ago nobody understood, nor suspected, the potentials of electricity. But they were there to be discovered. So is x x x x x.'

'So is – what?'

'Matthew has no word for it. It is a concept he cannot grasp.'

After a pause I asked:

'So you are here to sell us a new form of power. Why?'

'I have told you that. Intelligent forms are rare. In each form they owe a duty to all other forms. Moreover, some forms are complementary. No one can assess the potentialities that are latent in any intelligent form. Today we can help you over some obstacles; it may be you will so develop that in some future time you will be able to help us, or others, over obstacles. The employment of x x x x x is only the first thing we can teach you. It will liberate your world from a great deal of drudgery, and clear the way for your future development.'

'So we are, in fact, a speculative investment for you?'

'You could also say that if a teacher does not teach his pupils to overtake him there can be no advance.'

There was quite a lot more along these lines. I found it somewhat tedious. It was difficult to drag the conversation from the general to the particular. Chocky seemed to have her mission so much at heart. But I managed it at last.

Why, I wanted to know, out of, presumably, millions of possible hosts, had Chocky chosen to come here and 'haunt' Matthew?

Chocky explained that 'millions' was a gross overstatement. Conditions varied with the type of intelligent life-form, of course, but here there was a number of qualifications that had to be fulfilled. First, the subject had to have the type of mind that was susceptible to her communications. This was by no means common. Second, it had to be a young mind, for several reasons. Young minds, she explained, have absorbed so much that it is unlikely and inexplicable from myths, legends, fairy-stories, and religion, that they are disposed to accept the improbable with little question, providing it is not alarming. Older minds, on the other hand, have formed rigid conceptions of probability, and are very frightened by any attempt at contact: they usually think they must be going mad, which interferes with rapport. Third, it must be a mind with a potential of development – which, according to her, a surprising proportion have not. Fourth, its owners must inhabit a technologically advanced country where the educational opportunities are good.

These requirements narrowed the field remarkably, but eventually her search had brought her to Matthew who fulfilled all of them.

I said that I still did not see her purpose. She said, and I thought I could detect a note of sadness even through the flatness of the delivery:

'I would have interested Matthew in physics. He would have taken it up, and with me to help him he would have done remarkably well. As his knowledge of physics increased we should have had the basis of a common language. He would begin to understand some of the concepts I wanted to communicate to him. Gradually, as he learned, communication would grow still better. I should convince him that x x x x existed, and he would begin to search for it. I would still be able to communicate only in terms that he could understand. It still would be like' – there was a pause – 'something like trying to teach a steam-engineer with no knowledge of electricity how to build a radio transmitter – without names for any of the parts, or words for their functions. Difficult, but with time, patience, and intelligence, not impossible.

'If he had succeeded in demonstrating the existence of x x x x x – let us call it cosmic-power – he would have become the most famous man in your world. Greater than your Newton, or your Einstein.'

There was a pause while she let that sink in. It did. I said:

'Do you know, I don't think that would have suited Matthew very well. He hated taking the credit for saving Polly's life. He would have hated this unearned fame even more.'

'It would have been hard-earned. Very hard-earned indeed.'

'Perhaps, but all the same – Oh, well, it doesn't matter now. Tell me, why have you decided to give it up? Why are you going away?'

'Because I made mistakes. I have failed here. It is my first assignment. I was warned of the difficulties and dangers. I did not take enough notice of the warnings. The failure is my own fault.'

A scout, a missionary, she explained, should preserve detachment. She was advised not to let her sympathies become engaged, not to identify with her host, and, above all, to be discreet.

Chocky had understood this well enough in theory before she came, but once she had made contact with Matthew it had seemed that the preservation of detachment was not one of her gifts. Forms of engagement had seemed to lie constantly, and stickily in her path. For instance, after observing that Earth was a very oddly arranged and backward place, she had allowed herself to feel impatient with it, which was bad; and she had even let these feelings be known, which was worse. The proper missionary temperament would not have let itself get into arguments with Matthew; nor have been tempted into making disparaging remarks about the local inhabitants and their artifacts. It would simply have noted that Matthew was incompetent with his paints; it would have resisted the urge to try to help him do better. It would have been careful to keep its influence down to the minimum. Quite certainly it would not have permitted itself to develop an affection for Matthew that could lead to a flagrant interference with the natural course of events. It would regretfully, but quite properly, have let Matthew drown . . .

'Well, thank God for your lack of discretion that time,' I said. 'But are these indiscretions as serious as all that? I can see that they have aroused a certain amount of unwelcome attention, indeed we have suffered from it ourselves, but it doesn't seem to me that even taken all together they can amount to failure.'

Chocky insisted that they did. She had had her first suspicion that failure might lie ahead when Matthew had talked to Landis.

'He told him too much,' she said. 'It was not until then that I realized how much I had talked to Matthew. I could only hope that Landis would be unintelligent enough to dismiss it as a child's fantasy.'

But Landis was not. On the contrary, he had found it a fascinating problem. He had mentioned it to Sir William Thorbe, who also found it fascinating.

Chocky went on:

'When Sir William hypnotized Matthew, he did not hypnotize me. I could hear what Matthew heard, I could also watch through his eyes. I saw Sir William turn on his tape-recorder and heard him ask his questions. At first he was merely interested by Matthew's answers. Then he paid closer attention. He tried several trick questions. He feigned lack of understanding in attempts to catch Matthew out. He pretended to assume that Matthew had said things which he might have said, but had not. He tempted Matthew to invent, or to lie, with misleading questions. When none of these traps worked, he stopped the tape-recorder, and looked at Matthew very thoughtfully for some minutes. I could see him becoming excited as he accepted the implications. He poured himself a drink, and his hand was shaking slightly. While he drank it he continued to stare at Matthew with the half-incredulous wonderment of a man who has struck gold.

'Presently, with a decisive gesture he put down his glass. He took himself in hand and became coolly methodical. He re-started the tape-recorder, tested it with care, picked up a note pad and pencil, and closed his eyes for a few moments in concentration. Then the questioning really began . . .'

The Matthew-Chocky voice paused for a little.

'That was when I knew I had failed. . . . To attempt to go on further with Matthew would be a waste of time – and dangerous, too. I knew I would have to leave him – and would have to make the parting painful for him, too. I was sorry about that – but it was necessary for him to be utterly convinced that I was going for good – never to return. Nor shall I, after this.'

'I don't quite see . . .'

'It was quite clear that Sir William, having made his discovery, had his plans for making use of it; or handing on his news to someone else – and once that happened there would be no end to it . . .

'It did happen, and very quickly. Matthew was kidnapped. He was injected with hypnotic, and other, drugs. And he talked . . .

'They wrung him dry. Every detail, every word I had ever told him went into their tape-recorders. . . . And their recordings included his distress at my leaving him. . . . That was poignant enough to convince them that it was true, and under drugs it could not have been otherwise . . .

'They were not bad people. They certainly wished him no harm. On the contrary, until they learnt that I had left him, he was potentially a very valuable property indeed. They realized that he was a channel through which I could, when he should have more background knowledge and understanding, communicate information that would change the power sources of the whole world.

'When they had to accept the fact that I had left him, they decided the wisest course would be to let him go –

and keep an eye on him. They could always pick him up again if there were any sign that I had returned; and they will go on watching for that sign ...

'I don't know whether they have bugged this room yet, but if they haven't, they will. It doesn't much matter now whether they have, or not, because I really am going, after this.'

I broke in.

'I don't think I altogether understand this,' I said. 'From your point of view, I mean. They, whoever "they" may be, had Matthew. They could have seen to it that he should have the best possible coaching in physics and maths and whatever is necessary for him to understand you. That was what you wanted: your channel of communication – with all the help they could make available to him. If your purpose is, as you say, to tell us how to tap "cosmic power" you had the whole thing on a plate. They want to know what you want to tell them. And yet, instead of seizing the opportunity, you withdraw. ... It doesn't make sense ...'

There was a pause.

'I don't think *you* altogether understand your own world,' was Chocky's reply. 'As I said, once someone has told the news to someone else, there is no end to it. There is industrial espionage: there is also temptation ...

'There are power-empires: oil interests, gas interests, coal interests, electrical interests, atomic interests. How much would they be willing to pay for information of a threat to their existence? A million pounds ... two million ... three million ... even more? Somebody would take the chance ...

'And then what would a little boy's life matter? What would a hundred lives matter, if necessary? There would be plenty of effective ways of taking action ...'

I had not thought of that ...

Chocky went on.

'I tell you this because Matthew will be watched, and you may become aware of it. It does not matter, but do not tell him unless it is necessary. It is unpleasant to know that one is watched.

'If you are wise you will discourage him from taking up physics – or any science, then there will be nothing to feed their suspicions. He is beginning to learn how to look at things, and to have an idea of drawing. As an artist he would be safe . . .

'Remember, he knows nothing of what I have been telling you through him.

'Now it is time for me to say good-bye.'

'You are going back to your own world?' I asked.

'No. I have my work to do here. But this failure has made it much more difficult. It will take longer. I shall have to be subtle. They will be watching for me now.'

'You think you can do it in spite of that?'

'Of course. I *must* do it. It is my duty as one intelligent form to another. But now it will have to be done differently. A hint here, a hint there, an idea for one man, a moment of inspiration for another, more and more little pieces, innocuous in themselves until one day they will suddenly come together. The puzzle will be solved – the secret out, and unsuppressible. . . . It will take a long time. Probably it will not happen in your lifetime. But it will come . . . it will come . . .'

'Before you go,' I put in, 'what *are* you, Chocky? I think I might understand better if I could imagine you as more than a blank. Suppose I were to give Matthew a pencil and paper, would you have him draw a picture of you?'

There was a pause, but then it was followed by a 'No' that was quite decisive.

'No,' repeated the Matthew-Chocky voice. 'Even with my training I sometimes find it hard to believe that forms like yours can house real minds at all. I think you would find it still harder to believe that mine could if you could see me. No, it is better not.' The voice paused again, then:

'Good-bye,' it said.

I got up, feeling stiff and somewhat chilled. There was

a dim early light filtering through the curtains, enough of it to show Matthew still lying in his bed, still gazing blankly into nothingness. I moved towards him. His lips parted.

'No,' they said, 'let him be. I must say good-bye to him, too.'

I hesitated a moment, then:

'All right,' I said. 'Good-bye, Chocky.'

Twelve

We let Matthew sleep the whole morning. He came down at lunch-time, tired and subdued, but, I was thankful to see, not distressed. After lunch he got out his bicycle and went off by himself. We did not see him again until he came in weary, but hungry for his supper. Immediately he had finished it he staggered upstairs to bed.

The next day, Sunday, he was almost his usual self again. Mary's concern diminished as she watched him put away a prodigious breakfast. Polly, too, seemed to feel that things were back to normal, though something seemed to weigh on her mind. Presently she voiced it.

'Aren't we going to *do* anything?' she inquired, at large.

'What do you mean "*do* anything"?' Mary asked.

'Well, it's Sunday. We could do *something*. I mean, when Twinklehooves got back from being kidnapped they put on a special gymkhana for him,' Polly suggested hopefully.

'I bet he won all the events, too,' said Matthew through toast and marmalade.

'Well, of course. It was *his* party,' Polly said, fairly.

'No gymkhanas, or other jamborees,' I told them. 'Matthew and I are going to take a quiet stroll, aren't we?'

'All right,' said Matthew.

We took our stroll along the river bank.

'She told me she had to go,' I said.

'Yes,' agreed Matthew. He sighed. 'She explained properly this time. It was pretty horrid the way she did it before.'

I did not inquire into the explanation she had given him. He sighed again.

'It's going to be a bit dull,' he said. 'She sort of made me notice things more.'

'Can't you go on noticing things? The world's quite an interesting place. There's lots to notice.'

'Oh, I do. More than I did, I mean. Only it's kind of lonely, just noticing by yourself . . .'

'If you could get what you see down on paper you'd be able to share your noticing with other people . . .' I suggested.

'Yes,' Matthew admitted. 'It wouldn't be the same – but it'd be something . . .'

I stopped, and put my hand in my pocket.

'Matthew, I've got this I want to give you.'

I took out a small red leather-covered case, and held it out to him.

Matthew's eyes clouded. His hands did not move.

'No. Take it,' I insisted.

He took it reluctantly, and gazed at it dim-eyed.

'Open it,' I told him.

He hesitated. Slowly, and even more reluctantly he pressed the catch, and lifted the lid.

The medal glittered in the sunlight, reverse side uppermost.

Matthew looked at it with an indifference that was near to distaste. Suddenly he stiffened, and bent his head forward to examine it more closely. For some seconds he did not move. Then he looked up smiling, though his eyes were overbright.

'Thank you, Daddy. . . . Oh, thank you . . .!' he said, and dropped his head to study it again.

They had made a nice job of it. It looked just as if it had always been inscribed:

JOHN WYNDHAM

THE CHRYSALIDS

David Strorm's father doesn't approve of Angus Morton's unusually large horses, calling them blasphemies against nature. Little does he realize that his own son, his niece Rosalind and their friends, have their own secret aberration which would label them as mutants. But as David and Rosalind grow older it becomes more difficult to conceal their differences from the village elders. Soon they face a choice: wait for eventual discovery or flee to the terrifying and mutable Badlands ...

The Chrysalids is a post-nuclear story of genetic mutation in a devastated world, which tells of the lengths the intolerant will go to to keep themselves pure.

'Remains fresh and disturbing in an entirely unexpected way' *Guardian*

'Perfect timing, astringent humour . . . One of the few authors whose compulsive readability is a compliment to the intelligence' *Spectator*

JOHN WYNDHAM

THE DAY OF THE TRIFFIDS

When a freak cosmic event renders most of the Earth's population blind, Bill Masen is one of the lucky few to retain his sight. The London he walks is crammed with groups of men and women needing help, some ready to prey on those who can still see. But another menace stalks blind and sighted alike. With nobody to stop their spread the Triffids, mobile plants with lethal stingers and carnivorous appetites, seem set to take control.

The Day of the Triffids is perhaps the most famous catastrophe novel of the twentieth century and its startling imagery of desolate streets and lurching, lethal plant life retains its power to haunt today.

'One of those books that haunts you for the rest of your life' *Sunday Times*

'Has captivated readers for over half a century' *Guardian*

JOHN WYNDHAM

TROUBLE WITH LICHEN

Francis Saxover and Diana Brackley, two scientists investigating a rare lichen, discover it has a remarkable property: it retards the aging process. Francis, realising the implications for the world of an ever-youthful, wealthy elite, wants to keep it secret, but Diana sees an opportunity to overturn the male status quo by using the lichen to inspire a feminist revolution.

As each scientist wrestles with the implications and practicalities of exploiting the discovery, the world comes ever closer to learning the truth . . .

Trouble With Lichen is a scintillating story of the power wielded by science in our lives and asks how much trust should we place in those we appoint to be its guardians?

'Ingenious' *Evening Standard*

JOHN WYNDHAM

THE KRAKEN WAKES

It started with fireballs raining down from the sky and crashing into the oceans' deeps. Then ships began sinking mysteriously and later 'sea tanks' emerged from the deeps to claim people . . .

For journalists Mike and Phyllis Watson, what at first appears to be a curiosity becomes a global calamity. Helpless, they watch as humanity struggles to survive now that water – one of the compounds upon which life depends – is turned against them. Finally, sea levels begin their inexorable rise . . .

The Kraken Wakes is a brilliant novel of how humankind responds to the threat of its own extinction and, ultimately, asks what we are prepared to do in order to survive.

'Ingenious, horrifying' *Guardian*

He just wanted a decent book to read ...

Not too much to ask, is it? It was in 1935 when Allen Lane, Managing Director of Bodley Head Publishers, stood on a platform at Exeter railway station looking for something good to read on his journey back to London. His choice was limited to popular magazines and poor-quality paperbacks – the same choice faced every day by the vast majority of readers, few of whom could afford hardbacks. Lane's disappointment and subsequent anger at the range of books generally available led him to found a company – and change the world.

'We believed in the existence in this country of a vast reading public for intelligent books at a low price, and staked everything on it'
Sir Allen Lane, 1902–1970, founder of Penguin Books

The quality paperback had arrived – and not just in bookshops. Lane was adamant that his Penguins should appear in chain stores and tobacconists, and should cost no more than a packet of cigarettes.

Reading habits (and cigarette prices) have changed since 1935, but Penguin still believes in publishing the best books for everybody to enjoy. We still believe that good design costs no more than bad design, and we still believe that quality books published passionately and responsibly make the world a better place.

So wherever you see the little bird – whether it's on a piece of prize-winning literary fiction or a celebrity autobiography, political tour de force or historical masterpiece, a serial-killer thriller, reference book, world classic or a piece of pure escapism – you can bet that it represents the very best that the genre has to offer.

Whatever you like to read – trust Penguin.